CEDAR GREEN

A Selection of Recent Titles by Rose Boucheron

APPLE TREE COTTAGE
BIRCH COMMON
THE BUTTERFLY FIELD
CYPRESS GROVE
BY THE RIVER
FAREWELLS
FRIENDS AND NEIGHBOURS
PROMISE OF SUMMER
A SECRET IN THE FAMILY
SEPTEMBER FAIR

CEDAR GREEN

Rose Boucheron

This first world edition published 2008
in Great Britain and the USA by
SEVERN HOUSE PUBLISHERS LTD of
9–15 High Street, Sutton, Surrey, England, SM1 1DF.

British Library Cataloguing in Publication Data

Boucheron, Rose
　　Cedar Green
　　1. Cotswold Hills (England) - Fiction 2. Pastoral fiction
　　I. Title
　　823.9'14[F]

ISBN-13: 978-0-7278-6686-8   (cased)

All Severn House titles are printed on acid-free paper.

Printed and bound in Great Britain by
MPG Books Ltd., Bodmin, Cornwall.

One

E die Fisher was up early on that wintry morning. The sun streaked thinly across the room when she pulled the curtains and glanced up at the kitchen clock – time was important to her, although she had always been an early riser, had to be. The cleaning lady, they called her, although she preferred the term 'domestic', and she had done that all her life. Well, not when her daughter Mandy was small, but as soon as she went to school. Had needed to – Alf didn't earn much as a factory worker.

Mandy would be down presently – she would be off to work like her mother but a bit later in the day.

Today, Monday, was Mrs Hastings' morning – the job she liked least, but well, it was easy work and it had to be done. She worked several half-days a week in various houses and thanked her lucky stars that she was still able to.

In the kitchen she turned down the damper, and pulled down the door to the kitchen range, which gleamed almost like silver where she had blackleaded it over the years. A good poke through the ashes which fell below into the ash tray, fine grey ash, almost red hot at the top, then with a cloth to protect her hands, she took the ashes outside to pile up in a special corner of the garden. It was always fairly warm in this kitchen. The range supplied hot water to the tank behind, and once the front was down the orange fire glowed. There was an open fire in the front room, but she seldom used that – they tended to sit in the kitchen.

She had been born and bred in South London and christened Editha but everyone called her Edie. When she married it was to a man who lived and worked in Witney, Oxon., and they had brought up their small daughter, Amanda, in a small terraced house.

When Alf got promoted to foreman, they bought a small

Ford car and sometimes on Sundays went for drives around the Oxfordshire countryside. It was then they decided that when Mandy got married and left home they would try to find a small cottage in a village somewhere.

But it wasn't to be, and when Mandy had married and Alf had died, Edie sat in the evenings looking at the little car sitting outside by the pavement, and made up her mind to learn to drive.

She succeeded, as she did in most things, and before long, she was taking herself round the countryside eyeing the tiny cottage properties and hoping to find something within her means.

On Bedford Row, High Street, in Cedar Green, she found No. 6 up for sale, and lost no time going after it. It was much cheaper than the little house she lived in, although in need of a lot of decorating, but she was a dab hand at that. In fact there was not a lot she couldn't do, except what she called 'real man's work', and she was fortunate enough to find a real man right next door – a gardener, still working in his seventies, who was always on hand to see to broken pipes and fuses and things that didn't work. Jim Pettisham had lived in the village all his life.

She finished her tea, for she was due at Heron Court. It was the easiest job she had, but that didn't make it more likeable.

She could hear Mandy up in the bathroom, and presently she emerged looking as pretty as a picture despite the fact that she'd had a late night and was due at Ledsham House at eight thirty. Edie shuddered inwardly – she was glad she didn't have that job with Lady Ledsham and all – she could do without that.

'Well, you were late last night,' Edie said. 'Did you have a good evening?'

'Yes, super. There were four of us – Pat, Gilly, Rosie and me. It was great – we went to The Chequers.'

'Good, was it?'

'Yes.' She looked across at her mother. 'We'll go some-time, eh?'

'Yes – that would be lovely,' Edie said. 'Well, I'll be off now. See you later.'

Walking to Mrs Hastings' at Heron Court she thought

about Mandy, she was so pleased when she went out with her friends, but if only . . .

She sighed. Mandy had married at twenty-two. Steve was a nice enough young man – but the sad thing was that he had died at the age of thirty-one in a tractor accident, leaving Mandy bereft. Mandy had given up her small cottage on the outskirts of Stow, where Steve had worked on a farm, and moved in with her mother. 'What's the point,' she had said, 'of living separate lives? I miss Steve, and I know you miss Dad – so why not?'

Edie was glad of her company. She thought the world of her daughter and the feeling was mutual. A few months after Steve died, Mandy left the supermarket where she worked as a cashier, and elected to do domestic work at Ledsham House – renamed by his wife, Diana, after Robert Ledsham was given a knighthood.

'It's a beautiful place, Mum,' Mandy said, 'and the work is easy – they have two other women there – a cook, and another cleaner.'

Edie wished for something better for her daughter; she was lovely, well dressed, she spoke well, and had done quite well at school – but it wasn't for her to interfere. If Mandy was happy, so was she. And of course Mandy's son, Tom, was a delight to both mother and daughter.

Coming now to the outskirts of Cedar Green, Edie approached the great iron gates with the gold initials intertwined on the front of them. Pushing through and closing them carefully, she made her way up the drive, which was lined with bulbs and conifers. She could see her neighbour, the gardener – 'Petty', as he was always called – way in the distance and already hard at work.

She had heard rumours around the village after that poor man's death, Mr Hastings. He had died some time ago. Suddenly, whilst driving home. He had been such a nice man, which was more than you could say for Mrs Hastings, stuck up so-and-so – well, she was, everyone knew that. She paid a bit more than other people – that was to ensure that you stayed with her. Edie wasn't daft. And she had heard rumours that he had left a pile of debts – well, she wasn't saying anything. That's why people employed her, because they could trust her, and after all, it was none of her business. Just as long as she got paid.

She arrived at the front door and unlike most houses in the area, there was no barking of a dog. Most people kept dogs around here – stood to reason, for safety – but not Mrs Hastings. A dog would spoil her precious house.

She rang the bell and Mrs Hamlett, the live-in housekeeper, opened the imposing front door.

'Good morning, Mrs Hamlett.'

'Good morning, Mrs Fisher.'

Oh, yes, everything was very formal in this house.

She went into the kitchen to get changed and emerged in her cotton overall, changing her shoes, before making her way upstairs to the luxurious bedrooms in order to do the bathrooms 'on sweet', or whatever they called them. And there were enough of those – five. Beneath Mrs Hamlett's dignity to give them a good scour – but this great house, and him gone, she wondered what would happen. Poor man . . .

'Mrs Fisher, Mrs Hastings would like you to go at twelve today as she has some business people coming – rather important people, so if you could finish then . . .?'

'Of course,' Edie said. 'No problem,' and set about the bathrooms, which were immaculate; just a quick flick around the daughter's room. Poor lass. To lose a father. She had left school and had been in her gap year when her father died, but she had been so upset at her father's death, she had gone to Africa soon after the funeral, hoping to help out there and to solve some of her own problems. For there was no love lost between her and her mother.

Edie finished by cleaning the silver and brass – and there was plenty of that – cleared everything away and swept the yard outside. Mrs Hamlett paid her and she arrived at the gates just as a shiny black limousine entered with three or four important looking men in it.

Hmm. Well, there certainly would be a lot to sort out business-wise, she imagined.

She hurried back home, walking briskly, almost humming a little tune, and once inside picked up the post, mostly circulars, and cut herself a sandwich and made a pot of tea. This afternoon she was due at her favourite job – Mr Paynter's house near the church, Churchgate House.

It was a lovely old place, set back off the road, a small, eighteenth-century house with a delightful garden. It was the saddest thing that Mr Paynter's wife had died, leaving a little girl without a mother. She would be fourteen years old now, little Janie. Fortunately she had an auntie in the village – her auntie Barbara – and went to an excellent school.

Churchgate House was what Edie called a 'real' home. Furnished with such taste, while the garden was a dream. Both Mr Paynter and his wife had gardened, but apparently it was Mrs Paynter who had done most of it.

Unlocking the door, for she had her own key, she sensed there was someone in the house, and it turned out to be Mr Paynter's sister, Barbara Faulkner, who was the mainstay of the village.

'Oh, Edie – there you are. I was waiting to see you. Everything all right?'

'Fine – anything special you want me to do?'

'No, I don't think so . . .'

'Is Janie all right?'

'Yes, she's fine – got a music lesson this afternoon, so she won't be in until later.' She got ready to leave. 'I'd better fly – it's my afternoon book group. I'll be in again on Wednesday morning and you can let me know then if there is anything I can do. Lock up after you—'

'Oh, don't worry, I will,' and closing the door after her, Edie got down to work.

From an upstairs window in Ledsham House, Mandy saw Lady Ledsham step out of the chauffeur-driven Mercedes and walk with her two daughters to the front door. The chauffeur stood at her side with parcels and was there when Alice, the housemaid, opened the door.

Lady Ledsham really was a beauty, Mandy decided, for all her spoiled and fretful ways. How her husband had put up with her Mandy would never understand.

Now – she went downstairs, where Lady Ledsham stood in the hall talking to her two daughters, Sophie and Julia, who crowded around her like a couple of old hens.

Slowly taking off her gloves, a frown on her beautiful face – when was she ever without one? – Lady Ledsham looked frail. Mandy stood, waiting to help.

'I thought you were going at lunch time?' one of the daughters, Julia, said.

'I was to give a message to Lady Ledsham, that Sir Robert is coming in early – he is flying to New York this evening, and leaving for the airport late this afternoon.'

At this, Lady Ledsham sank into a deep armchair.

'Mummy!'

Lady Ledsham took a deep breath. 'Oh!' She placed a small hand to her heart, closing her eyes.

'Mummy, are you all right?'

Lady Ledsham sank into the back of the chair.

'Take my shoes off, darling,' and Sophie did so, placing the high-heeled, delicate shoes together at her mother's feet.

'Mummy, shall I call a doctor?'

The pained expression never left Diana Ledsham's face.

'No, no, it will be all right – my, legs, oh, and my back—' She writhed in what seemed like agony.

Waiting for an order, Mandy watched her. What a beautiful complexion she had; the long lashes sat on her cheeks like fans around a small nose, and when she opened her eyes, they would be large and violet coloured. Her mouth was a perfect shape, small and full – and she was, as far as Mandy was concerned, always ill.

Sophie leaned over her. 'Mummy – what is it?'

'It all right, darling. I will be all right in a moment. I am exhausted . . .'

'You shouldn't have gone,' Sophie said. 'It is exhausting going round the shops . . .'

'I had to,' Lady Ledsham murmured.

'Can I do anything, milady?' Mandy asked.

'No, thank you, I will be all right. You can go now, Mandy.'

'Then if there is nothing else . . .?' and Mandy made a move.

Suddenly the front door opened and Sir Robert came in, a tall, handsome man of some fifty years.

'Darling,' he said, placing his gloves on the hall table and throwing his newspaper down. 'What is it?'

'I feel so ill, Robert,' her Ladyship said.

'Have you called the doctor?' he asked, taking her wrist in his hand.

'No, I will be all right,' she said.

'Oh, darling,' he said, 'and I am off to New York this evening—' and her eyes opened wide with fear.

'Oh, no! But if you have to go . . .'

'I certainly won't go leaving you like this,' he said, taking her hand. 'Sophie, I think we should call the doctor.'

But Lady Ledsham had gone limp.

'Call him on the study telephone,' he said.

'Is there anything else, sir, can I do anything?' He glanced up at Mandy, who was hovering in the doorway.

'No thank you, Mandy – we will be fine,' he said. 'We will give you a call if we need you.'

Lady Ledsham moaned slightly.

'Hurry,' he said to Sophie, 'tell him it's urgent. I shall cancel my New York trip,' he said, 'see how your mother is.'

Lady Ledsham opened her eyes, fluttering her lashes. 'Darling, I'm sorry . . .'

'Don't worry, darling,' he said, patting her hand and getting his mobile phone out of his pocket.

Mandy crept away into the kitchen where she told Alice what had happened.

Alice said nothing but 'Oh, dear!', but she made no move to help.

Changing her shoes and putting on her jacket, Mandy left by the back door, walking down the drive.

There's one born every minute, she told herself.

When Mandy arrived home, Edie was preparing the evening meal.

'How did it go?' she asked.

Mandy took a deep breath. 'You'll never believe – Sir Robert came in – he was due to go to New York this evening – but oh, no!'

'What do you mean?'

'Her Ladyship came over all unnecessary, limp, exhausted, and he didn't like to leave her,' she said.

'But was she – I mean . . .?'

'Your guess is as good as mine, Mum.'

'Takes all sorts,' Edie said.

Two

Driving through the Cotswolds you could be forgiven for thinking that all these delightful villages are very similar, but you would be wrong. Each village has its own character and personality.

They vary, of course: some are distinctly up-market, while others still rely on farming – but they all have a personal charm. Each village has its own church and most of them have an interesting history. Sheep farming was the chief industry in the Middle Ages, hence the number of Sheep Streets and Lamb Streets you come across. With the passing years they have grown to cope with the admiring visitors who come by the thousand every year to enjoy the sights of the Cotswolds. Most have delightful hotels, one if not more; the shops are a joy to visitors seeming to stock the sort of things they cannot get at home. There are always other villages to explore, and Cedar Green is one of the most charming.

In Oxford, John Paynter stood looking out of his office window to the small courtyard where frost still shone on the lawn and a large tub of snowdrops in bloom gave the first hint of the spring to come.

As a solicitor running his own practice, John always looked suitably alert, his handsome face inspiring confidence, but now it softened as he saw the white flowers shining in the winter sunshine. John's wife, Lyn, had planted them twenty years ago when they first moved to Cedar Green, and what better legacy could his beloved Lyn have left him?

One last look and he made for his desk. Unfortunately his first appointment was with a woman who was not one of his favourite clients. The staff in the outer office were already there, the files were on his desk. Vanessa Hastings was due at eleven – that was the earliest she could manage. He had some bad news for her, and if he was honest with himself it was news that gave him a little pleasure.

Vanessa was a beautiful woman in her forties, elegant, and recently widowed – the wife of his friend, Stuart Hastings. He was aware that some people in the area thought it quite possible that he and Vanessa might make a go of it now that their partners had gone, but it had never been an option, at least not for him. He disapproved strongly of her lifestyle, and privately thought his friend Stuart had made a mistake in marrying her.

Early in June, Stuart Hastings, a City stockbroker, had been returning home to Cedar Green when a heart attack had sent him careering off the motorway, and he was dead by the time the ambulance reached him. He had never been ill in his life.

The Hastings' lived on the outer edge of Cedar Green in a Georgian house set among trees and surrounded by beautiful grounds. Since they had moved there on their marriage they had spent a fortune on the place, conservatories, extensions, laying out the grounds – Heron Court was regarded as one of the main attractions of Cedar Green.

John knew the cost of all this as Stuart struggled to cope with Vanessa's extravagant demands, and knew long before Stuart did that he was piling up trouble for himself.

Vanessa was stunning – no one could argue with that. Beautiful – she had style, and wore the finest couture clothes; they had plenty of staff and entertained extravagantly. Even with Stuart's position in the City John knew it would have to end sometime.

He had expected something of the sort when Stuart died. He had pushed himself too far – or Vanessa had, with her constant demands for more. His money was not inherited. All his wealth was made from City deals – and sometimes he overstepped the mark. As a close friend, John knew he was stressed out, but Vanessa either didn't see or refused to acknowledge her husband's limitations. Now he would have to tell her, after this long harangue over probate, that her lifestyle was over. She would have to leave Heron Court now that the party was over, so to speak.

He was waiting for her when Sheila, his secretary showed her in.

Those large, sorrowful dark eyes, he wouldn't deny that

she looked as wretched as he had ever seen her, dressed entirely in black, her pearls gleaming against the ivory skin.

He went forward and kissed her lightly on the cheek. 'Sit down, Vanessa – how are you feeling?'

The tears sprang easily, as he knew they would, but then she was genuinely upset. Her wonderful life was coming to an end. He had given her notice some two weeks ago of the prospects.

'Will you have coffee?'

She shook her head impatiently.

'Oh, John,' she cried, dabbing her eyes. 'I don't think I can bear it!'

He studied her. 'You have had a terrible shock, but Vanessa you must be brave. You are strong—'

'Me?' And the tears came. 'Then you don't know me very well – I just can't cope with this.'

'But you will,' he said, 'because you have to and you are a practical woman.'

'Oh, how can you possibly understand?' she cried. 'A man has no idea!'

He regarded her steadily.

'Oh, I'm sorry – I'm not thinking straight,' she said. 'Poor Lyn . . .'

He went round and patted her shoulder, deciding the sooner he got this over with the better.

'I gave you a hint a week or so ago, and I am afraid the news isn't good.'

Her eyes now were narrowed with suspicion.

'What do you mean?'

'You are going to have to sell Heron Court,' he said carefully.

She sat up straight.

'I am not joking, Vanessa,' he said. 'Stuart has left so many debts that I am afraid—'

'But that's not possible!' she said. 'He said nothing to me about debts . . .'

'He wanted to protect you,' John said gently.

'How cruel!' Vanessa said. 'And what about Sarah? What will she do? The university fees, I mean?'

'Your accountant will deal with everything,' John assured her. 'As your solicitor, I'm dealing with the legal side of things.'

She eyed him suspiciously.

'You realize that the legacies and so on that he left to various people mean nothing now – there is no money. What you own personally will be yours, but the sale of the house, of course, will be used to pay off debts – of which there are many. This has been coming for a long time.'

'Why didn't he tell me?' she sobbed.

'He was trying to protect you. After all, he had no idea that he was going to die so soon.'

She buried her face in her hands. 'Oh, how awful – what will happen? Where will I go?'

'The bailiffs will have to come in, the house and contents sold to defray debts – except anything that belongs to you personally, as I said. Stuart owned no other property, as far as I know. It is a case of bankruptcy.'

She covered her face with her hands. 'Oh my God! Will everyone have to know?'

He had it in his heart to feel sorry for her. It was an awful thing to go through, no doubt about that.

'Do you have any relatives?' he asked her. He had no doubts at all that she would land on her feet. People like her always did.

'A brother,' she said, 'in Canada, but I never see him . . .'

'Well, I will do my utmost to help you in whatever way I can. No need for me to tell you how deeply sorry I am. Stuart was my best friend.' And he felt his throat constrict.

But she wasn't interested in his feelings. Giving a great sigh, she got to her feet.

'What happens next?'

'You will be hearing from your accountant – and don't forget, Vanessa, I am on hand if you need any help.' He held out his hand, but she ignored this, and made straight for the door, where she turned.

'I may seek further advice on this, John,' she said.

'As you wish, Vanessa,' he said, closing the door after her.

He sat thinking for a time after she had gone. Nothing would change the fact that Stuart had gone and left an empty place in her life. And a pile of debts. He could only imagine how Vanessa must feel.

Half an hour later, a knock came on the door, and Sheila entered.

'Mrs Farrell is here,' she said.

'Oh, thank you – show her in, will you, Sheila?'

He got up and went towards the door, holding out his hand, and saw an attractive woman, possibly in her late thirties, wearing blue jeans and a leather jacket. How he hated women in jeans!

'How do you do – Mrs Farrell, is it?'

She took his outstretched hand and there was, he noticed, a look of amusement in her eyes. Most clients, on first meeting, had a look of apprehension.

'Laura Grey.' She smiled. 'Not Mrs,' she said, 'I am divorced.'

'Do sit down,' he said.

She made herself comfortable, easing off her jacket, and smiled at him.

'And how may I help?'

'I was given your name by a friend of mine – Janet Weatherall. You may know her – she lives in Cedar Green, as I believe you do.'

He smiled, but he hated any reference to his private life, which to him was sacrosanct.

'I do indeed,' he said, and knew he sounded stuffy. 'And where are you from?' He knew they would have the address outside, but they seemed to him to have started on the wrong foot. He was used to people being serious, and this young woman seemed to find life amusing.

'I live in Belford,' she said.

'Ah,' and he waited for her to go on.

'I had better start at the beginning, hadn't I?' And her wide grey eyes looked into his dark ones and he noticed a momentary hesitation as she prepared to go into details.

'I am thinking of moving,' she said, 'since I have seen something I would like to buy in Cedar Green.'

He felt a very little, he told himself later, a small, sharp stab of interest as he waited for her to go on.

'The thing is,' she said apologetically, 'it's like a step in the dark . . .'

So she wasn't as sure of herself as she made out. He gave what he hoped was an encouraging smile, and sat back, placing the tips of his fingers together.

'Well,' and she took a deep breath, 'I don't know if you

have noticed but in Cedar Green there is a small shop on the corner of Tinkers Lane which used to sell bits and bobs – gifts for tourists, that sort of thing. It has been closed for some time, and the lease is up for sale . . .'

Is that all? he thought

'Have you contacted the agent for the property?' he asked. This small stuff was hardly his cup of tea.

She frowned. 'Of course. And I have made an offer which has been accepted – but there is a fourteen-year lease to run and since I have never dealt with a lease before, Janet thought I should have some advice.'

'May I ask what you would use the shop for?'

'Antiques,' she said.

He wondered – did she mean *antique* antiques, or second-hand car-boot stuff? She didn't look the sort of person who would deal in rubbish, for apart from the jeans she was quite superior looking – a lady, he thought, using the old-fashioned term.

Now she looked at him, begging him to understand and give his permission.

'Have you had experience of this sort of thing – a shop, perhaps a business of any kind?'

She shook her head.

'Taking a bit of a risk, aren't you?' And he smiled to soften the words.

'Not really.' Her head went up. 'I am used to dealing with antiques, not selling them exactly – but I have always been interested since I was quite young. I studied Fine Arts, and did a stint at Sotheby's for a time.'

'And you think that is enough experience to enable you to open a shop?'

John thought he began to understand why her husband had left her: headstrong – or had she left him?

'There really is a lot more to opening a business than you might imagine,' he said gently.

But she had regained her composure. 'Oh, I am going to do it – if it is possible. If I don't do it now I never will. I am forty this year, Mr Paynter.'

An honest woman – that made a change.

'You say you have made an offer which has been accepted – what are you going to do about your own property – let it?'

'I wish,' she said fervently. 'No, I have to sell that in order to buy this – but of course there will be a differential.'

'Have you children?' John asked.

'A son of nineteen, Jamie, in his first year at university, so I thought, here's my chance.'

'Could I ask you – how long you have been divorced?'

'Four years,' she said, looking straight at him.

'And just the one child?'

'Yes.'

'How does he react to the idea?'

'Oh, he's all for it. It will give me something to do, he said.'

Yes, he's off to make his own life, John thought, wondering how he would feel when the time came for his daughter, Janie, to leave home. But she was only fourteen.

'One of the most important things – and I am assuming that your own house is freehold? – is that with a fourteen-year lease, when it runs out you will own nothing.'

'Perhaps they will extend it,' she said.

'That's wishful thinking – and hardly ever happens. Have you thought about that?'

'I don't worry about the future – you know, let it take care of itself.'

'Well, if that is your thinking . . .' he said. 'But there is much more to this opening a shop thing than perhaps you have imagined. Have you thought much about the actual buying and selling – the hours you will have to put in?'

'Well, I shall live on the premises.'

'You seem to have it all worked out.'

'It is quite a little home, Mr Paynter. There are two bedrooms and a bathroom upstairs, and downstairs behind the shop quite a large living room and kitchen, a pretty little garden – I shall like that.'

'You won't have much time for gardening,' he said dryly.

He could see now that however he argued, she was not going to change her mind. She was intent on it. Perhaps it had been a dream for a long time. Best to go along with it.

'Well,' he said, 'practicalities.'

She listened.

'Presumably you have asked the agent about the heating – and the water supply and all that? If it is to be your home . . .'

Her eyes shone. 'You really think I could do it?'

'I am not going to encourage you – but I can see you are determined.'

'Oh, I am.' She clasped her hands together. 'I can see it now. Decorated and filled with family furniture, a few small bits and pieces—'

'Do you know about pricing?'

'Oh, yes, indeed. I've watched the market ever since I can remember.'

'As long as you realize that you will have to take enough money each week to justify the purchase of the shop – with the overheads—'

'But I will have something from the sale of the house.'

'True, and it is fair to say that if you are going to live there it needs to be a real home as well as a shop. Be sure that the heating is OK. I can't recall the past people there – not a shop I went into, in fact.'

No, she thought, I can see that – the poorer end of the High Street, you might say.

'So your offer for the shop has been accepted. What about the sale of your own property?'

'I know someone who would like to buy it, and unless anything unforeseen happens it should go through without any trouble,' she said.

'You will have to buy the stock at sales or auctions – I have no idea where you go for that sort of thing – but then, with antiques it is the carriage and deliveries. You would need a van, presumably.'

'Yes, of course.'

'And while you are out at auctions and the like, who is in the shop?'

'Well, I thought I would close on Mondays and Saturday afternoons.'

He smiled. 'Tourists to the area are particularly keen on Saturday opening. And another thing, there is, as I am sure you know, a rather excellent upmarket antiques shop at the other end of the village.'

'Cattlins?' she said. 'Oh, I am no threat to them, nor they to me. They deal in only the best of French and Italian furniture. I am fond of old English myself.'

There was no stopping her.

He was curious now, for he could see she was determined.

'You would need to decorate it, it could do with a renovation, unless I am mistaken—'

'Well, of course, I'm a dab hand at decorating.'

'I see. Do you have friends who would help you?' He stopped as he wondered, Why am I getting immersed in this thing? It's never going to happen.

'You see, I have quite a bit of furniture that belonged to my parents. I have never had room to show it off properly, and I could start with that. Furniture has always been my first love. At Sotheby's I worked a lot with china and porcelain, but that's not my scene.' She was thoughtful. 'Silver, too. I don't know much about silver but I could learn.'

'A part-time assistant?' he suggested.

'Could I afford it?' Then she brightened. 'Mr Paynter, I am absolutely determined to see this through, despite the difficulties, and I am not silly: I do realize it is not going to be easy.'

One born every minute, he thought, as she got to her feet.

'So would you look after things for me?' she asked prettily, picking up her gloves.

'Yes, of course, if you wish,' he said stiffly, going to the door with her.

As she passed the window, she glanced into the garden.

'Oh, how lovely! Snowdrops.'

No one, John thought, had ever mentioned them before.

Three

Driving home from the city of Oxford towards London, leaving the busy streets filled with cyclists, elegant spires and colleges – a city which seems to be entirely populated by young people – John Paynter made for his home in Cedar Green.

A few miles on, he came to a left turn, St Martin's Lane, the signpost reading 'Cedar Green'.

St Martin's Lane slopes very slightly downhill, sheep still graze on the farmlands and the hedgerows on either side are dry and blackened on this winter's day. A farmhouse is passed on the way, a few cows nearby, and John Paynter never tires of driving this road, winter or summer.

At the end of the lane he turns right in to the village, Cedar Green, where stands St Martin's Church. On the small green is a large cedar tree, origin unknown. Had it been one of the seeds brought to England in the seventeenth century? It has been there as long as anyone living can remember, and there are several seats dotted around it on the green. Coming to the centre of the village, there is the church where St Martin's Lane joins forces with the High Street, the church where John's grandfather was vicar for nearly thirty years, while his father had been born in the vicarage which stood nearby and is now the village hall.

When John had married Lyn they came to live in Cedar Green, and bought Churchgate House, surrounded by a lovely garden they both adored. They had been undergraduates together at an Oxford college. Lyn also read law and came from Wimbledon in London.

The house was a joy, with enough to do to keep occupied in their spare time. But when Lyn died at the early age of forty-four, John had been devastated, not only for himself, but for his daughter, Janie.

No, he was fortunate to have his sister Barbara, his elder by some six years, living near by in a cottage facing the green, called May Tree Cottage. Barbara, a widow, was known for her good works in the village, for she ran everything, from the dramatic group to the horticultural society, the children's union and the art appreciation meetings. Janie adored her auntie Barbara, though she treated her more like a grandmother than an aunt.

He was also fortunate in having Edie Fisher to help him run the house. Three half-days a week she came in and was available to help him out with any extra work if she could fit it in. Edie thought she was the luckiest woman alive to have found this job, for she loved Churchgate House and the village and could turn her hand to anything. Edie was never one for an idle life.

If John had ever thought of remarrying he had never given any signs of it. He had plenty of friends and business acquaintances and entertained, after a couple of years, much as he and Lyn would have done. Now, five years after Lyn's death, he was used to being single again. He had a house he loved, a sister who lived nearby, and of whom he was very fond, and a daughter whom he adored; he felt he should be grateful for small mercies.

He came to a stop in the driveway which led to his home and contemplated the village as it was on this late Monday afternoon, dark now, although soon the nights would be getting lighter . . . He had been set thinking by the arrival in his office of the odd little woman Laura Grey. Was she mad or what? he wondered, using Janie's jargon.

He parked the car, and decided to take a turn around the village. There was no doubt it was an attractive little place. He walked towards Tinkers Lane, passing the green and the cedar tree which everyone took for granted. There was a small hotel – The Golden Lion – which he often popped into for a meal or a drink; a grocer's shop, now called The One-Stop Shop; a second-hand bookshop – heaven knew what Max Brooker did in the winter without tourists; a sixteenth-century house which had been lived in by a rich merchant and was now a B&B and neighbours had to admit it was kept very well, usually with plenty of flowers outside in the summer, small conifers and bay trees in the winter.

The baker baked excellent bread, but there was a rumour that he was closing down since business was bad. These days most people drove into Oxford for supermarket shopping and the market where everything could be bought, from bread to clothes and shoes.

He walked past the row of six cottages called Bedford Row towards Tinkers Lane and there the corner shop stood as always. With its old brown paint it was quite an eyesore in the village, though it had potential. It was a corner shop, therefore it had two windows which was an advantage, one in Tinkers Lane, and one in the High Street. A central door, boarded up now, shutters pulled. There was no point in trying to see inside, for there was no way he could. He walked to the side door, which was in Tinkers Lane, locked and bolted, which obviously led to a small garden.

He couldn't think of a more depressing project – it was at the dull end of the village – did the tourists venture that far?

Coming out of the lane into the High Street, he faced the setting sun, and strolled glancing into the shops: the chemist's, which was run by his good friends, a couple from Scotland, Bob and Margaret McAllister; he glanced into the dress shop – he knew nothing about that except that he had negotiated the buying of the business for the proprietor, a pretty woman from London, Greta Nelson. Next door was a coffee shop, owned now by Italians; the one charity shop in Cedar Green; a men's shop, the signboard read 'Robert Doughty – Gentleman's Outfitter'; a gift shop, then the estate agent's. Sheep Street intervened at this point, and across the road was a general store. Fewer things stood outside in this cold weather and he was coming now to what was deemed the nicer end of Cedar Green. The White House, a very elegant Georgian house, well looked after, with a beautiful garden and tall stone tubs, filled now with pansies and violas. A widow lived there – she had inherited the house from her husband and was quite the most exalted person in the village. Lady Somerville was her name and few people saw her out and about. She was driven everywhere when she went out, which was not often.

He was now coming near to the exclusive antiques shop owned by Dirk Cattlin, reputedly a Belgian – and glanced in the window. Now here was genuine antique stuff. He and Lyn had often admired the beautiful things he had for sale, but they were usually beyond their reach money-wise, and not really suitable for their home.

He hurried back towards Churchgate House, where he put his car away in the garage and opened the front door, where the warmth and welcome smell of cooking filled the hall . He disappeared into the cloakroom where he washed his hands and peered at his face in the mirror – and wondered, unusually for him, how he appeared to other people.

In the kitchen he found a note from Edie Fisher which read that she had left a casserole in the oven and all he needed to do was to turn it off when he was ready, a salad and a sweet were in the fridge. Janie had a music lesson and would not be in until later, as she was going to have supper at her friend's house.

In the dining room, he poured himself a glass of whisky which he usually had at the end of a day, and took it into the drawing room, which they seldom used. Janie spent a lot of time in her room, while he worked in his study.

Before he pulled the curtains, he looked out to where more snowdrops stood in tubs – they were a welcome sight in the winter. He remembered he and Lyn had sat in the college garden at Oxford knowing that whatever happened they would ultimately marry.

When Lyn saw Churchgate House for the first time she had been enchanted.

'You know what's missing?' she had said, holding his hand tightly. 'A strawberry tree.' And they had laughed, and searched for one in the nurseries around. It had been small then – now, fifteen years later, quite a tree to be reckoned with. Strawberry tree, he thought. *Arbutus Unedo.* The fruit, once tasted, you would never try again. Later they had bought another for his office courtyard . . . in early summer, the white flowers came, then later the little bitter-tasting strawberries.

He would never forget his Lyn, he thought. The snowdrops and the strawberry trees would remind him – she had been such a gardener.

He had finished his meal and stacked the dishwasher when the tapping of a key on the glass panel of the front door meant that his sister Barbara was about to enter. He would be pleased to see her and to enlighten her as to the future of the little corner shop. They would have a laugh, and it was great to have someone to talk to.

'Cooeee!'

'Barbara! Everything all right?'

'Yes, I just thought I'd pop over and check – where's Janie?'

'Music lesson and gone to tea with Linda – they'll drop her home.'

'I thought you might like a drink?'

'Good idea,' John said, going over to the drinks cupboard.

'It's a lovely evening, John.'

He smiled, handing her a glass of wine. 'How is it all going? With all your activities?'

'You know me – I like to be busy.'

'You might be interested in this little bit of news – I had a new client in today who is interested in buying the little corner shop in Tinkers Lane.'

'Oh, that will be great! It's such a dead corner. What's it going to be?'

'Can you believe it? An antiques shop.'

He knew his sister well enough to know she never spread gossip around the village, she was like his Lyn in that respect.

'What a joke! Opposition for Cattlins, eh?'

'I hardly think so. She's never done it before – I have to say I think she's biting off more than she can chew ...'

'Bit risky,' Barbara agreed. 'Still, that will be nice. That corner needs livening up – not a rubbish shop, is it?'

'No – I don't think so.' And he laughed. 'Nice woman, if a bit batty.'

'Where does she come from?'

'Belford.'

Barbara's blue eyes widened in surprise. 'What's her name?'

'Laura Grey.'

'I believe I know her!' Barbara cried, eyes shining. 'Oh, good for her! I've met her at art appreciation meetings – oh, and other places . She comes to see Janet Weatherall.'

'Who's she?' John asked. 'She mentioned a Janet Weatherall, said she had given her my name.'

'Lives in Rydal Mount – married to George Weatherall.'

'Oh, the business tycoon.'

'Yes, but she is nice – they are friends, she and Laura. Oh, good for her. I'm so glad, that end of the village could do with brightening up – is it all settled?'

'No, a few things to sort out but she seemed absolutely adamant about what she proposes to do.'

'She has a son,' Barbara mused. 'Nice lad – I suppose he would be about.'

'At university,' John said.

'Oh, so she is free to do what she wants. She is a divorcee.'

John stared into the distance, hating to admit he was curious, and forbore from asking why. Barbara would tell him if she had a mind to.

'She comes to the book club sometimes,' Barbara said. 'And the Oxfam meetings.'

'Well, I've never met her before,' John said, as if to close the subject.

Barbara shot him a glance.

'She's a nice woman, John,' she said at length.

He went over and poured himself another drink as if he hadn't heard.

It was late when the phone rang in Laura Grey's house in Belford.

'Laura Grey,' she said, wondering who was calling so late.

'Janet,' the voice replied.

'Oh, hallo, Jan.'

'I'm really sorry to bother you so late in the day, but I've only just got back from town and I couldn't resist asking how you got on with John Paynter.'

'Oh, fine – he was very helpful.'

'Oh, didn't pooh-pooh the idea, then?'

'No – why should he?' Laura sounded surprised.

'Oh, I don't know, after all he is there to advise you against taking risks.'

'You think it risky? In what way?'

'Oh, come on, Laura. It's your first venture – it could be fraught with problems.'

'So I'll deal with them when I come to them. It's not like you to be so downbeat, Jan.'

'Well, I've been a bit worried about you.'

'You have? I thought you encouraged me!'

Janet laughed.

'How do you know John Paynter?'

'He was my father's solicitor.'

'Oh – that figures.'

'What does that mean?'

'Nothing – what are you doing tomorrow?'

'Nothing in particular, why?'

'I thought I might come over and if I get the key from the agent we could go over and look at the shop.'

'Super idea. What time?'

'About eleven? I'll call for you.'

'Bye then, see you tomorrow.'

True to her word, Laura called for Janet around eleven.

'Shall we go first to the shop and come back afterwards for coffee?'

'Good idea,' Janet said. 'We'll need warming up.'

They drove to the other end of the High Street and parked.

'Well, I must admit it looks as if it needs putting back on the map,' Janet said, getting out of the car.

Laura fished for the keys the agent had reluctantly given her as they made for the door.

'Yes, I can't wait to get on with it.'

She unlocked the door and let them in, and the stale smell of dust and emptiness assailed them.

'Phew!' Janet said. 'I wouldn't know where to begin.' But the light of battle was already in Laura's eyes.

'You know, it gets better every time I see it. I can't wait,' she said.

It was a decent sized room with plenty of window space, being on the corner, and Laura raised the window blinds, for the electric light was not on.

'I brought a torch just in case we were in darkness,' she explained.

With a stretch of imagination you could see that it could be turned into quite a nice shop, stripped, painted and decorated.

'What's under that disgusting carpet?' Janet asked.

'Disgusting wood, I expect,' said Laura cheerfully, as they walked through the door to the small passageway and into the kitchen.

Janet opened a door at the side.

'Oh, that's handy – a cloakroom.'

'And in front of you is the kitchen,' Laura said.

'God!' Janet said. 'You're going to need a completely new kitchen.'

'Why not?' Laura said airily. 'After all, it's going to be my home as well as my business. I shall look forward to that.'

'It'll cost you,' Janet said.

'So?' Laura knew she was being flippant but underneath her warm coat her heart was beating fast with excitement.

There was an outside door to the garden, and in the corner a small shed.

'Now – *that* will be useful.'

'For stacking your fine English furniture?' Janet quipped.

'You can sneer all you want, but that's a dear little garden – someone has grown bushes and plants.'

'Not a sign of colour anywhere.' But when Janet looked at Laura's face, which was flushed, her blue eyes shining with excitement, she had a sudden feeling of guilt.

You had to hand it to her – her life hadn't been easy.

There were two bedrooms upstairs of good size and a bathroom which also would have to be modernized. Still, Janet thought, rather Laura than me – but then she's got guts, had to have after that swine of a husband left her.

But she was better off without him – and she had Jamie, which was more than Janet had.

'Come on,' she said suddenly, 'it's freezing in this place – let's get us some coffee. I'm frozen.'

And locking up securely, they hurriedly made their way back to the car.

Four

Far away in the city of Rome, Graziella Massini was sorting through her mother's possessions. The apartment was colourful and filled with costumes and headdresses; the silk curtains were overabundant and draped to the floor; there were gilded tassels, pictures and photographs everywhere; and soft carpets from the East, for her dear mama had been a much-travelled lady. Although the apartment was not on the Via Veneto, it was nearby in the Via Spoleto.

Her beloved mama had died three weeks ago, and now Graziella, who had shared the apartment with her in the last year, was having to go through her possessions.

Graziella was a beautiful woman, as beautiful as Italian women can be, and very like her mother, who had been an actress. She was tall and slim, with abundant dark hair and enormous dark eyes, one look from which was capable of reducing a man to a lovesick swain or a blithering idiot.

But she had had her share of men, and now at the age of twenty-nine was trying to imagine the way ahead.

She had done her share of acting, too, but she had not the gift her mother had possessed. She had married into the most prestigious of societies, the Roman elite, but the women were wary of her. One extra-marital affair and she was ousted, not because of the affair – most of them had those – but because she had been stupid enough to be found out.

So – which way now?

The trunk in front of her revealed her mother's most treasured possessions, photographs from her early days as an actress, film stills, and here a picture of her own darling father.

Graziella smiled to herself and hugged the photograph to her. How handsome he had been. She had adored him. But he was a daring man – motor racing, winter sports – and had left his rather prestigious home in England to come and live with her mother in Italy. He had died when she was eighteen – was it all those years ago? A heart attack – and who would have thought it in such a man? – on the slopes at Chamonix. Both she and her mother had been inconsolable, but life had to go on. Dear Mama had picked up the threads – and continued with a life as colourful as she could make it, bringing up her daughter as well as she knew how, which was not easy given her daughter's temperament.

Arguments and rows, blissful reconciliations – life had always been hectic. But now? The future looked bleak.

In a strong box, she found her mother's birth certificate, licences for this and that, government forms giving permission for various things, then at the bottom of the box – her own father's death certificate.

He was English – that much she knew; no wonder her mother had fallen for him. And he for her, apparently, else why had he left his own country to settle in Italy with her? Had he ever been back? Not to her knowledge. She had never been herself; she had been to the USA, all over Europe – but never to the United Kingdom.

Now, with Mama gone, she must make the best of her life.

There were more photographs, of her parents together in exotic places. Sometimes she was with them, as a growing child, a teenager. She leaned back and remembered wonderful journeys they had made together, how proud she had been of them, for they were a handsome couple. Her mother had been a beauty – men were mad about her – and she was fortunate that she had inherited her mother's good looks.

Now, in this black strong box with a brass clasp, she found what she imagined to be the really important papers.

Her mother's birth certificate: Julietta Massini, born in Naples in 1952; her own birth certificate. She had been born in Rome, on 27 June 1977, mother Julietta Massini – father unknown.

She gasped out loud and the colour left her cheeks. What did this mean? Father unknown? Her father was English – David Graham Somerville, that had been his name, although she herself was known as Graziella Massini – always had been. She had never queried it. She brought out more papers.

There was no marriage certificate but she had known that there wouldn't be. Her mother's passport, certificates of vaccination – and at the bottom two envelopes. The first contained a dark blue passport, British, embossed with gold, and inside a picture of her father as a young man. Inside were the particulars. David Graham Somerville – and an address in England. His parents were Eustace Somerville and Celia Somerville. The passport had been stamped many times. He was a British citizen, born in England in 1948. She turned the black box over and here on the side were his initials in gold – D.G.S.

And now for the second envelope, which was thick and white, addressed to David Graham Somerville, at an address where they had once lived in Florence.

She withdrew the notepaper, heavily embossed in black, with an address and a brief handwritten note.

Lady Celia Somerville
The White House
Cedar Green
Oxfordshire
> *Your father is dead. Please do not write again.*

A scrawled signature followed: *Celia Somerville.*

The tears rushed to Graziella's beautiful eyes. Her father must have written to his mother and received this reply – he had died without ever seeing his father again. He must have loved him very much. It was unbelievable – this wretched woman! That people could be so cruel – and her mother had been such a sweet and lovely person. Why did they disapprove? Was it because she had been an actress? That was ridiculous. But then, all this was fifteen or twenty years ago – twenty-nine years if you counted from when she was born.

The tears having started, which was unusual for Graziella, she let them run freely, sobbing now, for her mother's death, and for the sorrow her father had endured, and because she was alone. How cruel life could be.

She read through everything once more, then packed the papers carefully away. She felt stiff when she stood up – and drained. Exhausted was the word, but she made fresh coffee, thinking all the while.

By the time she went to bed, she knew what she was going to do.

* * *

Graziella woke early with the events of the night before upper-
most in her mind. She hadn't changed her thinking at all. She
took her time over breakfast, cleared away and watched the
sun's rays shining on the roofs of Rome, the spires, the palaces,
the elegant buildings, and sat herself down at her mother's
desk.

Taking a sheet of paper from the holder with its address
clear at the top, she began.

> *Dear Lady Somerville,*
> *I take pleasure in writing to you, for I believe that*
> *you are the mother of my late father, who died eleven*
> *years ago.*
> *Now my dear mother has died also, and I am plan-*
> *ning a visit to England to see where my father was born.*
> *Life is so very short – and it is a matter of sadness*
> *to me that we have never met. Cannot this be rectified?*
> *I will be coming to London sometime in the spring, and*
> *I would very much like to meet you.*

She read what she had written. She had no intention of bowing
and scraping to this woman who would probably not answer
her letter, anyway.

She continued.

> *My father was a wonderful man, and I loved him dearly.*
> *Do say you will agree to a meeting.*
> *Kindest regards,*
> *Graziella Massini*

She read it through a few more times before sealing it. She
would post it tomorrow. It was a good idea to sleep on it.
She might feel differently tomorrow.

Father unknown indeed!

Tuesday morning was Edie's day at Lady Somerville's house.
She went just one morning a week, since her Ladyship
employed a live-in housekeeper, and Edie was employed to do
'the rough' work. If she objected to this she never complained,
for the rough at The White House was hardly dirty work.

The house was kept immaculate by Mrs Baker, but Edie

enjoyed her work for The White House was pleasant, elegant, and with just Lady Somerville and Mrs Baker there was nothing the house needed except a general going over. Edie did the silver, the dusting of ornaments, the polishing of floors with an electric polisher. There was also a woman who came in to do the laundry one day a week, and very efficient she was too.

Edie enjoyed her work and got on quite well with Mrs Baker, although she seldom saw her Ladyship. She was usually in her bedroom or the drawing room. In the summer, she spent a lot of time in the garden, and Jim Pettisham worked there as well as the gardener, had done for thirty years, but he was getting old now, and a younger man did the heavy work.

On this particular morning, a warm winter's day, that indicated spring was on its way, Lady Somerville sat in the study, a room much used by her husband when he was alive. She was seventy-eight years old, and had been widowed when she was quite young.

She was a good-looking woman with white hair which she pulled back from her face into a knot with hairpins; a patrician nose; intense, heavy-lidded blue eyes, somewhat faded now; and a well-shaped, firm mouth. She had been quite a beauty in her day and was conscious of her position, for her husband had been knighted by the Queen for services to his country.

She was at her desk staring in front of her, seeing nothing, with memories coming to life, vivid memories. These had been brought back to her by the letter she had received the day before which she had thrust away from her, only to read it and re-read it again and again. Something restrained her from tearing it to shreds, which she had wanted to do. Also, she had not wanted Mrs Baker to see it in the waste-paper basket, even though she felt like screwing it up, burning it. Instead, she had put it under the blotter on the desk.

Now, all the colour gone from her face, she stared in front of her. After all this time – strange how the past caught up with you.

All she could see was the darling, adorable little boy, her pride and joy, as they played in the gardens of the house in Worcestershire where they had lived before coming to The White House, which her husband had inherited. As an Eton schoolboy they had gone to see him, then he had gone out into the world.

He was such a nice little boy, adored by everyone that knew him – but that had been his downfall. Whatever he wanted he thought he could have. Including that ghastly Italian actress – he must have been mad. All the girls were after him, that was half the trouble.

Of course, she knew what had happened over the years, had made it her business to know. Knew where he lived, when he had his daughter, when he died. Oh – what a terrible time. He had been so young – she had kept to her bed for days, and told no one. She doubted if anyone remembered that she had a son, it was all so long ago.

And now this.

She read it for the umpteenth time – how dare she? A girl no better than she should be, from what she had gleaned from her two special, intimate friends who kept an eye out for her.

Coming to England, was she? Well, she would see about that! A short note refusing to see her would scotch that. Grimly, she read the letter again. The writing was good, but then all Europeans wrote well. And it was brief and to the point. So the girl was on her own. She was a woman now, must be almost thirty.

She admitted to herself the curiosity which consumed her, but it was not to be even considered. Nothing good would come of it. What was the woman after – money?

She looked across at the cheery fire blazing away in the study. It would take but a moment to see the letter reduced to ashes – and yet . . .

She slipped it under the blotter again as Mrs Baker came in, bringing her coffee and biscuits on a tray.

'Quite chilly out, milady,' Mrs Baker said. 'And there is a bit of a wind.'

'Yes.'

'Have you got some letters you want me to post this morning?'

Lady Somerville started. 'No thank you.'

'Edie's here – if you want any shopping done—'

'No, thank you.'

When the door closed behind her, Lady Somerville sipped her coffee and read the letter again. She was mesmerized, still as surprised as she had been when it arrived.

Carrying the letter she took her coffee over to the window and read it again.

What if she were to—?

But no. A firm no. Heaven knew what she might start up if she replied. Did she really want to see this Italian woman? Heavens, no! But David's daughter – that was the rub. And really, what was there in her life to look forward to? She had been lucky to get this far, when she thought of some of her friends who had died before her. She no longer went away on holidays – it was all too much of an effort, her legs were not too good – and what lay in front of her but the same old thing? And she was one of the lucky ones. Bridge with a few friends, the occasional dinner party, small but enjoyable. She didn't walk far these days.

Suppose – but no, the idea was not worth thinking about.

If she did agree to see her, who knew where it would end . . .

Yet – she was her only relative, the last Somerville. Whatever she was like, she was that.

It came over her suddenly, the desire to see this woman. She was a blood relation. Her granddaughter – how odd that sounded – and she was just asking to visit her. What harm was there in that? Impulsively, she took a sheet of writing paper from the rack, and before she wrote the letter addressed the envelope to the flat in Rome.

Graziella Massini – so she wasn't a Somerville. What was the reason for that?

But by now curiosity had got the better of her. She would not make it personal, neither would she sign herself as the woman's grandmother. Was she married – divorced? That much she had never found out. Her interest had been in her son.

Finally she began.

> *Dear Graziella Massini,*
> *Thank you for your letter.*
> *I understand you are coming to England sometime this year. Perhaps if you would get in touch with me nearer the time we can arrange for you to pay me a visit, but give me plenty of notice. I live a very quiet life here.*
> *Yours sincerely,*
> *Celia Somerville*

She wasn't going to mention the mother. Certainly not.

Having read it through a few times, she finally sealed it, and called in Mrs Baker, placing the letter under the blotter as usual.

'Mrs Baker, would you ask Edie to come in for a moment?'

'Is anything wrong, milady?'

'No – everything is quite all right. I want to see her for a moment.'

Edie was quite shocked to be called into the private domain of her Ladyship.

'Your Ladyship?' she queried, thinking everything at once, how old the old lady was looking, unwell almost, but there was a light in her eyes, almost a twinkle.

'Would you do something for me and post a letter?'

'Of course, your Ladyship,' Edie said.

'I don't think it will be more than a pound, so I will give you two pounds, just to be sure – I don't know what the postage rate is to Italy.'

'No problem,' Edie said, and took the letter and put it into the deep pocket of her apron.

'Anything else, milady?'

'No – that will be all.'

No need to tell Edie to say nothing to anyone. Edie knew how to keep a secret, and that's what it was, for sure.

'Everything all right?' Mrs Baker asked, eyeing Edie suspiciously, waylaying her as she was going out through the kitchen door.

'Yes, fine,' Edie said. 'Cheerio then, Mrs Baker.'

'Bye then,' Mrs Baker said, her lips pursed in a straight line.

When Edie reached home she found Mandy by the fire, sobbing as if her heart would break.

Edie hurried over to her.

'Mandy! What is it? What's wrong?'

Mandy buried her face against her mother's bosom as Edie's arms went round her.

'Mum, Mum – it's Robert' – she heaved a great sob and tried to pull herself together – 'Robert – he's dead. Mum, he's dead!'

'Mandy!' Edie held her close. 'How—? I mean, what—?'

'Collapsed, heart attack and died,' Mandy said, sobbing.

'Oh, Mandy, little love, oh, Mandy – what will she do?'

'As if I care!' Mandy said, drying her tears. 'Oh, Mum – he was so young – while she with her bloody tantrums—'

'I know,' Edie soothed, 'I know, love.'

She smoothed Mandy's hair, staring into space.

It was a long time since she had done that.

Five

O h, what a night that had been! She and Mandy had stayed up until the small hours talking about it. It didn't seem possible – Sir Robert, dead – and he was so young. What did the future hold? for Mandy? for Lady Ledsham – her family?

Edie was off in the morning to Churchgate House after she had seen Mandy off. Barbara called in as she usually did, and of course the talk was all of the tragedy at Ledsham House. Thank goodness Edie had the afternoon to look forward to.

Tuesday afternoons were strictly reserved for the Women's Guild.

She really looked forward to that, could recall her mother going way back in the days when they lived in London and thinking, Catch me doing that when I grow up! But here she was, looking forward to it.

She looked at her calendar on the kitchen wall, and saw that a Dr Sadie Thompson was to speak on the best way to keep healthy as you grew older, which should be interesting, although what with TV and magazines and radio, all you ever heard today was on the subject of health and losing weight.

Sadie Thompson – that rang a bell. Didn't that writer, wonderful man, Somerset someone-or-other – she would remember it later, didn't he write a story about a Sadie Thompson? She recalled getting it out of the library – she always remembered his books. Had read all her life. Her mother had called her a bookworm. 'Always got your nose in a book.'

Yes, Sadie Thompson – that was her name. Something to do with a missionary, and at the time it had seemed a bit – well, rude, but so well written. She sat thinking. She had gone to school with a girl called Sadie – Sadie Green, she was her best friend. They used to walk home together from school, well, them and a girl called Rose. Rose was as unlike Sadie as it was possible to be. For one thing she was good at maths, or arithmetic as they used to call it at the elementary school in South London. Both Rose's parents were teachers, and socialists, her mother had said with disapproval, although at the time Edie never knew what that meant. Rose was tall and wore glasses, had thin hair, and just tagged on to them.

Sadie was the dunce of the class. She knew nothing, but she was great fun. She was shortish, pretty, with black curly hair and rosy cheeks.

She had farther to go on the way home from school than either Rose or Edie, down to the High Street, where her father had a tailor's shop. 'A. Green, Bespoke Tailor', it said, and the shop was divided in two. Edie could see it now. The left hand one had shelves with bolts of material, and Sadie's father, a dapper little man, was well respected. Edie's father used to wish he could have a suit made by him but he could never afford it, and went to the fifty-shilling tailor's instead.

The other side of the shop was for women's wear. Lots of shelves with underclothes, silk knickers and stockings, and Sadie's mother sat there, knitting, waiting for customers. Her name was Bertha and she was pretty, like Sadie. Black curly hair, black horn-rimmed glasses, very well dressed. Sometimes when Edie went home with Sadie, with her mother's permission, of course, she would go through Mrs Green's shop, then through the kitchen and outside to where a brick building housed several workers – machinists, ironers, cutters – but Edie could never understand a word they said. They used to stare back and smile at the two small girls.

'Where do they come from?' she asked Sadie one day.

'Lithuania, I expect,' Sadie said, and grabbing Edie's hand went back into the kitchen where a young woman was making tea.

'Where do your parents come from?' Edie asked one day, for she realized they were not English.

'London, silly,' Sadie said.

'But way back—'

'Russia, I think.'

One day, on one of her visits to the shop, Sadie's mother looked hard at her.

'She's very thin,' she said to Sadie. 'Are you anaemic?' she asked, turning to Edie.

Edie had never heard the word before.

'No,' she said.

'Well, you look as if you need feeding up,' she said. 'Next week I give you some borsch. You know borsch?'

'No,' Edie said.

'Best thing for growing young girls,' she said. 'Beetroot soup – you know?'

Edie shook her head.

She could remember it all as if it were yesterday. She didn't tell her mother, for she knew she would disapprove, but the following week, Sadie's mother handed her a big jug full of dark red liquid. 'So I put a lid on for you,' she said, 'and don't drop it on the way home.'

Edie clutched the jug tightly.

'Tell your mother to give you some every day, and bring the jug back when you have finished.'

Edie went home with misgivings.

'What's this?' her mother frowned.

'Mrs Green – Sadie's mother – gave it to me,' Edie said.

'For what?' she asked, still frowning.

'It's good for you – she said I am too thin.'

Her mother compressed her lips.

'You don't need this,' she said. 'Did you thank her?'

'Yes,' Edie said

Edie sat, staring into space. All those years ago . . . They were eleven and took the Junior Supplementary, if she remembered correctly. The Eleven-Plus came later. Sadie failed miserably, but Edie did well enough to go to a central school where she learned French and typing and lost all contact with Sadie.

She got up, sighing, and cleared away the lunch things. She often wondered about Sadie and what happened to her. She could have gone to a trade school and learned a trade – perhaps she took over her mother's shop.

She rinsed the things under the tap – Sadie had been the best friend she'd ever had. And whatever had happened to Rose, the girl with the brains?

Well, enough of that – my goodness, look at the time! She must get ready.

Putting on her cardigan, she made her way down the High Street and into the church hall.

There was quite a crowd there as usual, and they all nattered a bit before taking their seats, and after the usual announcements from Barbara Faulkner, the chairman, she announced the speaker for today.

'It is with great pride,' she began, 'that I present' – and out from behind the curtain, stepped – 'Dr Sadie Thompson!'

Edie gasped.

She couldn't believe her eyes! It was Sadie Green! She would know her anywhere. Older, of course she was – her black hair still curly but grey; behind those glasses dark eyes, warm, smiling eyes; a white blouse and beautiful tweed suit – lovely brogues; she was shorter than Edie remembered, but she looked just like her mother, Bertha. By now Edie was almost in tears.

'I know her!' she wanted to shout, 'I was at school with her!' but of course she didn't.

She hardly heard the lecture which Sadie gave, she was so overcome. Sadie – a doctor! How could she be? She hadn't even passed her Eleven-Plus – or whatever it was called back then. How had she managed to pass all those exams – this pretty little woman who spoke so nicely without the trace of a south London accent? And it *was* her.

Edie was almost in tears – her mind full of schooldays when she was young.

When it was over there was great applause – although Edie's heart was beating fast. She would go up to talk to her after the meeting – several people would want to – it was something Edie seldom did, but today was different.

She waited until the tea break when they sat having tea and cakes, Dr Sadie Thompson was probably in the little room behind the hall, but she would see her later. There were several other items to be discussed, but since Barbara Faulkner hadn't joined them, she judged that Sadie had stayed behind to talk to her in the little room.

And then Barbara emerged. Edie's heart pounded.

'Now, I am sure you all enjoyed that wonderful talk by Dr Thompson, and ladies, we are all going to eat sensibly and by the time we see Dr Thompson again we will be slim young things after all our exercise . . .' Oh, get on with it! Edie thought irritably.

'Now, if any of you have queries or would like a word with Dr Thompson she would be pleased to answer your questions.'

A huge bouquet of flowers was handed to her, then Sadie sat herself at the little table, and waited for the few people who wished to ask her questions.

Edie kept out of the way until the last one had gone – there were five – and then she made her way carefully up the three platform steps and walked towards her.

Sadie's wonderful smile greeted her, but by now Edie was almost shaking – but slowly, Sadie's smile turned to wonder as she searched her memory – and stared open-mouthed.

'Dr Thompson,' Edie began in a croaking voice, and Sadie – née Green – opened her eyes wide.

'It isn't—' she began, 'it's not – Edie – Hallowell!'

Edie nodded, choked.

'My dear!' and Sadie got up and put her arms around her, while looking over at Barbara's puzzled face.

'An old school friend,' she said, looking as pleased as punch.

She stood Edie away from her.

'You look wonderful,' she said. 'And you don't look as if you need any help from me!'

Edie nearly burst with sheer pleasure.

'Why don't you go into the little back room – you can be quiet there and talk over old times.' Barbara smiled.

Barbara wasn't a bad old thing, if bossy, decided Edie.

Arm in arm Sadie and Edie left the room.

'Well!' they both said together and giggled like the school friends they had been.

'What are you doing in Cedar Green?' Sadie asked.

'I live here,' Edie said, almost proudly.

'No! Well – that's a turn up for the books!' Edie caught a trace of the old London accent. 'I've just moved here.'

'No! Where – in Cedar Green?'

'No, not quite – just outside in Farthingale Lane. I'm staying with my son who is renting a house in Farthingale Lane. I am retired now, and a widow . . . And you?'

'Me too – a widow, that is. I'm not retired,' Edie said.

'Who would have thought we would meet up again as a pair of widows,' Sadie said. 'My son, you know – no, of course you don't! Well, I have a son – Daniel – and he is

about to buy a local property – and if it is suitable, I may go
and live with him. Have you children, Edie?'

'Yes, a daughter.'

'How wonderful. Daniel is divorced – and I hope he gets
the house he wants, then I shall be living near you.'

How nice she was, thought Edie. No showing off, no 'side',
as they used to say.

'Has he found a house yet?' she asked.

'Well, he has had particulars sent to him – and he is
interested but he hasn't seen it yet.'

'Is it local?' Edie did hope Sadie would come to live near
her.

'Yes, it's called Heron Court – do you know it?'

Edie gasped. 'I work there,' she said proudly.

'What?' Sadie asked. 'What do you do?'

'Housework,' Edie answered proudly, but inwardly she was
ingesting Sadie's words. She knew nothing about the house
being up for sale, but true to her nature she said nothing.

Now, Sadie was curious. 'Tell me, what is it like? Is it large
– he wants a large house.'

'Oh, yes, it is very large,' Edie said. 'Beautiful,' for it was.

'Is it?' Sadie sounded quite excited. 'Sounds quite grand –
Heron Court.'

'Oh, it is.' Edie smiled.

'What are the people like who own it?'

'Charming,' Edie said. 'The husband died recently – a car
accident – last year.'

'Oh,' and Sadie nodded. 'That's why they are selling then.
I'll tell Daniel I have met you and our history – it's wonderful,
isn't it? I am so glad I agreed to come today.'

'Do you do a lot of this – lecturing?' Edie asked.

'Well, I hope to now I have retired. I quite enjoy it – think
of the rewards it brings!' and they laughed together.

'Now you must give me your address and telephone number
and I will give you mine, except that it is temporary, of course.
I don't quite know where I shall end up.'

Edie couldn't believe any of this was happening but was
delighted that it had, then had a premonition that Sadie might
ask her to show her the house.

'I don't know your married name – Mrs—?'

'Fisher.'

'Do you drive?'

'Yes – but not today. I live quite near.'

'Then come in my car.' Sadie sounded excited.

'Come where?' but she knew what the answer was going
to be.

'Show me Heron Court.'

But Edie knew she was not going to get involved at this
stage. She glanced at her watch.

'Sadie, I'm sorry – I can't today, I have to get back. But
look, I'll give you my address and telephone number and you
can ring me.'

'Oh, never mind.' Sadie sounded disappointed. 'No
problem.'

'What does your son do?' Edie asked.

'He's a property developer,' Sadie said.

They hugged each other.

'Now – keep in touch,' Sadie said. 'Sure you don't want a
lift?'

'No – I live just down the street.'

'See you soon, then.'

A property developer . . .

John Paynter was just going to lunch when his secretary
announced that Vanessa Hastings hoped she could see him for
a moment.

He glanced at his watch. Typical of Vanessa.

'Show her in,' he said to Sheila.

She looked far more pleasant than the last time he had seen
her. She was actually smiling and holding out her gloved hand.

'John – how nice of you to see me. I know you must be
awfully busy, but I thought I would call in and tell you the
news.'

It hadn't occurred to her that he might be in touch with
other people regarding her business.

'Sit down, Vanessa – nice to see you. How is it all going?'

Judging by her smile, very well.

'Well, John,' and she removed her gloves slowly, 'Heron
Court is on the market – and I think I have someone interested.'

'That's good news,' he said pleasantly.

'Well – it had to be done,' she said, as if it were her idea
in the first place. 'I do realize the situation and after all, what

would I be doing in such a huge place as Heron Court? I have a life to lead, too, you know,' and she looked at him sadly from large brown eyes. 'The agents suggest around two million – with the land.'

'Yes, I daresay – well, they would know,' John said. 'And you say you have some interest?'

'So the agents say.'

'Well, it will all go towards paying the debts.' She frowned. 'It was a wise move, buying Heron Court.'

'Well, that was my idea,' she almost pouted.

'Now – how can I help you?'

She smiled again. 'Well, just keep doing what you have to do, John. It is early days yet.'

'And how is Sarah?'

'I don't hear a lot from her – you know what the young are like.' She began putting on her gloves. 'Perhaps we could have dinner some evening, John?'

'That would be nice,' he said, as she got to her feet, and walked her to the door.

She turned and kissed him briefly.

'Thank you for all your help, John – I do appreciate it,' she said.

'My pleasure,' he said, and closed the door after her.

Six

There were five large and beautiful black hats at the funeral of Sir Robert Ledsham. Seated at the back of the church as she was, Mandy Davis could not help but see them, and she wondered idly who they were. The church was crowded, as was to be expected of such a famous and popular man. Struck down in his prime, so to speak – although his prime had been going on for some years now.

Mandy had considered her right to be there at all, as the Ledshams' cleaning lady, or daily woman, whatever they called her kind today. But still, she had wanted to pay her respects. He was a lovely man.

They could be female relatives, Mandy supposed, perhaps sisters, or wives of business tycoons. It was a very well-dressed funeral, as indeed it should be, him knowing all those important people, and that.

One of the hats turned slightly, and showed a perfect profile, a dangling earring, a lovely face and Mandy looked down at her own outfit. Well, navy was the next best thing to black, and it was such a fine day – it seemed all wrong somehow to be sitting in church for a funeral.

You could have knocked her down with a feather when she had arrived last Wednesday morning and been told that Sir Robert had died the night before, suddenly – a heart attack, the housekeeper, Mrs Carey, had told her. Well, it was a good way to go. Still, not very nice for them as were left behind. Not that she had much sympathy for Lady Ledsham, Sir Robert having made this year's honours list. Oh, she'd been pleased all right – like a cat with two tails. She'd had them calling her milady in no time.

Ah, now here she was, Lady Ledsham. Mandy turned her head. Small, looking frail – though she wasn't – she was as tough as old boots, escorted on either side by a daughter. Lots of women in that family, she thought, two daughters, and one granddaughter – and there they were, all little beauties – and not a boy amongst them . . .

Still, she looked nice. Neat, extremely pretty. A black-and-white print silk dress, small becoming hat, a wisp of white blonde hair curling beneath it. They'd been married a long time – she would be lost without him. Still, she'd survive. She was a survivor, that one. Mandy herself would never had stayed on, but she liked the family, the girls, and the house-keeper, and the work was easy. Such a lovely house, a bit like Howards End.

Funny thing, Mandy thought, today was her birthday. Funny to be going to a funeral on your birthday. Still, when her husband died she had been only thirty-one, and she had carried on working at the supermarket, but when someone told her about working up at Ledsham House – Mrs Ledsham had called it that – she applied and got the job. The hours were good and suited her, and the money she could do with – she had her widow's pension – and besides, she found the work quite pleasant.

As for him, he was a lovely man. So good-looking, tall, well built, very nice grey eyes he had, with a sort of twinkle in them – a nice nose, and his hair, grey now, or was, but still thick, grew to a point, a widow's peak, she thought they called it. And a mole just beneath his left eye. Oh, yes, he was a handsome man all right. And she – Lady Ledsham – had held on to him, she had been lucky, but her rule was law. She ruled him, they said, with a rod of iron . . .

Oh, now came the vicar, and the coffin carried by eight strong men, a polished coffin with brass handles that shone in the sun's rays coming through the stained glass windows. On it, sprays of flowers – and Mandy swallowed hard. Oh, it was so sad.

And now the organ sounded and they got to their feet.

The girl with the black hat and earrings bit her lip, and the tears sprang unbidden from very blue eyes. She was his private secretary. Twenty-nine years old, and she knew that life would never be the same again. No more trips to the States, those wonderful hotels, the intimacy of those luxurious bedrooms, New York, Los Angeles, Chicago.

She had been his mistress for five years, having started with the company when she was twenty-four, but it hadn't taken long. She adored him. Of course her family disapproved, but she had gone her own way.

'Old enough to be your father,' her mother had said in disgust, while her father just looked upset whenever she saw him. So she stopped going home.

Robert had taught her so much not only in a business way, but how to live life to the full. She had her own flat – paid for by Robert. Would she – dare she wonder? – had he made any provision for her? His death was so sudden. She wiped a surreptitious tear away with a linen handkerchief.

That could be a niece, Mandy thought.

Susan Leadbetter sat next to her husband. Entirely in black, the large black hat pinned back off her face with a black rose. Her husband was – or had been – Robert's best friend. Jack Leadbetter and Robert Ledsham had started out together as partners, and as the business grew and expanded, each had become very wealthy. Homes in the country and in London, a place in Italy – and in all that time, Jack had never suspected. She glanced at him now, seeing his face, his large square face, flushed now with genuine sadness, in his eyes a fear as to who would be next. Her lip curled slightly and she took a deep breath as he glanced at her, and she gave him a thin smile. He took her hand and pressed it gently then took up the hymn sheet as they rose to their feet.

Jack was a weak man, she thought – sometimes she had prayed that he might find out about her and Robert, that it might bring at least some excitement to her marriage, but it had been left to Robert to do that. God, what a man. And what would she do without him now?

And that silly little woman who thought she knew all the answers – standing there, her daughters beside her – and she breathed hard. Oh, Robert, Robert.

Mandy thought she recognized Mr Leadbetter – she had seen his picture in the papers – and that must be his wife next to him, she looked a hard-faced so-and-so.

Hilary Denning stood up slowly, her firm, sturdy legs encased in their black opaque tights, flat shoes. She had worn a hat, partly to shield her face and because she hoped no one would recognize her, but never had she felt so ridiculous. Ladies golfing champion, all those wonderful weekends over now, Gleneagles, the Scottish weekends – she must have been mad to come. Robert was the only man she had ever really loved. She had never seen his wife before, let alone his family – what a shower . . . she hadn't imagined her like that. And those girls – his daughters – somehow she had never really thought about his family. When she and Robert were together – rarely enough – they had enjoyed every moment. His family had never really entered into the scheme of things – but here they were in the flesh, so to speak. Well, she just had to pay her respects and she would be off and away, together with this blasted hat which she couldn't wait to take off.

Fancy all these people, Mandy wondered. So many – the church was full, as the voices rang out everyone seeming to put their heart and soul into it. When they sat down again, Mandy took another look at the woman in the large black hat some two rows in front of her. She seemed to be alone. So elegant, small, and wearing a black silk suit. Hair upswept underneath her black hat, which was enormous. Pearl earrings – she must be about, what, fifty, sixty? She wasn't young

Madeleine Dessart had come from Paris. Quite simply to be with her lover of some fifteen years. Her perfect English lover. She had felt her heart break when she heard the news. And of course, there were others – but only one Robert. How proud she was to be seen with him whenever he came to Paris. That wonderful brief holiday in the Seychelles – where he had ostensibly gone on business. Oh, but he was naughty! Naughty Robert – but still, she was lucky. That unobtrusive little woman must be his wife – how had she held on to him?

He had been faithful to her in his fashion, and Madeleine smiled to herself. Well, over the years, however brief, she had been the one in his life who had consoled him for what was obviously a very boring marriage. Could English women be anything but? she asked herself. It took a Frenchwoman to understand a man.

Very elegant, Mandy thought – she didn't look English, somehow.

Gwen Harrison sat beneath her large black hat, quietly crying. She had come all the way from Nottingham, leaving her two little girls in the care of her mother. It was a long time since Robert had come to Nottingham for a conference and needed a stenographer urgently. She had been freelancing then, working as a temp.

Oh, what a handsome man he was! She had fallen for him hook, line and sinker. But he had been fair, told her that he was happily married, and had no wish to leave his wife, but she had quite literally thrown her bonnet over the windmill.

She hadn't cared. He had set her up in a little house, seeing her when he could, which lately was not often, but she had settled for that. Twin girls had been born six years before, and he had been more than generous. With her promise that she would never reveal their secret, she had been more than happy to settle for what she had. She lived comfortably, her two little girls' education was provided for. Her mother said that now that he was dead, perhaps Gwen would find someone.

'No,' she had said firmly. 'There would be no one like him, not ever,' and her mother sighed.

The eulogy was being read, and now it was over, they rose again to sing another hymn.

Afterwards, Mandy got ready to leave, and saw Lady Ledsham bearing down the aisle, escorted by her daughters and their husbands, of course. All good-looking, as a family. She wondered how she would manage. Would she give up the house? Would Mandy still be required?

To avoid being seen, she looked down, at her plain navy skirt and jacket. Well, she had been a good-looking woman herself once. Someone had once said with those dark eyes she looked a bit like Norma Major. Well, she didn't want to catch Lady Ledsham's eye. Perhaps she would have disapproved of her coming. Well, blow that.

'Come on, Tom,' she said to the lad beside her, and smoothed his hair which grew thickly and in a widow's peak. His nice grey eyes, with that mole just beneath the left one adding a bit of interest. Yes, he was a nice-looking boy – the only male Ledsham – and off to public school next year.

Oh, yes, she had a right to be here and to pay her respects, as Lady Ledsham, her of the pretty face and petulant mouth, moved down the aisle surrounded by pretty daughters . . .

Oh, what a successful man, she thought. All those people.

They crowded into the drawing room at Ledsham House. Never had there been so many people present at the reading of a will.

Many of them had received explanatory letters – not surprisingly, for Sir Robert had been a very methodical man, and not the sort of man to leave knots untied or any room for doubt.

For of course, it was well known that Sir Robert was a very rich man indeed. Millions, some said, but figures these days sometimes seemed mythical. The room was crowded, and Mr Dennison, Sir Robert's solicitor, and his assistant, Bates, were very much in charge. Chairs had been brought in from every room, although Lady Ledsham reclined rather than sat, pale as a lily, never opening her eyes, it was such a foregone conclusion. She was flanked on either side by two pale-faced daughters.

Mandy was there, having been requested to attend and wishing she could be anywhere but.

Having cleared his throat, you could have heard a pin drop as Mr Dennison started reading.

'The Last Will and Testament of Robert Charles Ledsham . . .'

Bequests to servants and employees, there were thousands of pounds involved, the list was endless. Ten thousand pounds each to the hat ladies. Lady Ledsham did open her eyes at that point and then narrowed them at these bequests – who were these women? – but she tried to console herself. Previous secretaries – past and present – he had been a very busy and successful man. To his daughters, large bequests. Lady Ledsham had no fears until she heard the words: 'A bequest of five hundred thousand pounds to Mandy Davis, née Fisher, mother of my son, Thomas Charles Ledsham' – and she opened her eyes wide then fainted.

There was a general kerfuffle around Lady Ledsham, and when the murmur had subsided, Mr Dennison continued.

'Ledsham House to be maintained and kept in trust for my son, Thomas Charles Ledsham, until he reaches the age of twenty-one. All the contents of Ledsham House and my house in Italy I bequeath to my widow, Diana Frances Ledsham, together with the residue.'

Having surfaced, the Ledshams looked around for Mandy, but she had taken advantage of the lull, and fled.

'Oh, my God!' Edie Fisher said when Mandy arrived home, white and shaking. 'Where's Tom?'

'Gone back to school.'

'Whatever did her Ladyship say?'

Mandy shook her head. 'I didn't wait to find out, I just ran, but I've got a letter here—'

'Give it here,' Edie said, and easing it open began to read it, and read it through to the end.

'Half a million,' she said, 'and his school fees already paid.'

And the back door opened and in came Tom, his face as open and honest as any twelve-year-old's should be.

'Hi, Mum, Gran,' he said, and dropped into the large cane chair by the fire.

Mandy kissed the top of his head while Edie looked down at him and bit her lip.

'Hi, Tom,' she said. 'No football this afternoon then?'

'No, not today, Gran,' Tom said. 'Could I have my tea now – I'm starving.'

'Course you can,' said Edie, and ruffled his hair.

He wasn't short of affection in that house.

After dinner when Mrs Carey had cleared away the dishes, Diana Ledsham remained at the table. Dabbing her mouth delicately with her napkin, she put her elbows on the table and faced her daughters.

'I am leaving this house,' she said.

'Mummy!' Julia cried. She got up and began to go over to her.

'Sit down,' her mother said. 'I have made my decision – although it wasn't difficult,' she added dryly. 'The decision was made for me.'

'Where – where will you go?' Sophie asked, her lip trembling.

'To Italy – at first,' Diana said. 'As you are both aware, this house has been left in trust and therefore belongs to us. I have no further use for it, but you and your families may come and spend time here. The expenses will be paid and the staff, Mrs Carey and the gardener, kept on – everything as usual, but I will not be here. I shall go to the house in Italy and from there probably to France. I will keep in touch – you will know where I am.'

Why was she being so hard on them? Sophie wondered. They had done nothing – it was as if she was cutting them all, her family, out of her life altogether. Perhaps this was just a temporary blip, something she would review again when time passed and the blow softened. There would be no point in arguing with her.

'You have your own lives,' Diana went on, 'and I have mine. If there is anything you would like – any furniture, anything at all in the house – please take it. The house will not belong to us in a few years so there is no point in keeping it.'

'Mummy – does that mean we will never see you?' Julia's eyes were wide and bright. Sophie had to feel sorry for her. She had always been closer to her mother than she herself had.

'Oh, please think it over,' Sophie pleaded. 'You shouldn't do anything hasty – it's too soon—'

Her mother turned cold eyes towards her. 'And what would you know?' she asked. Her eyes were like flint, her fine nostrils flared, her soft, pouty mouth set in a grim line.

'When do you think you will be leaving?' Julia asked.

'As soon as I am ready, my dear,' she said coldly.

As they watched her leave the room, Sophie had tremendous pity for her. What a blow she had just had – no woman could take that. Perhaps they should be pleased that instead of falling apart, she had garnered strength from somewhere to make her own decision. That she was cutting herself off from everything that had to do with her husband was obvious. How bitter a blow must it have been. And a maid servant in their house – a cleaning lady – oh, she was more sorry now than she thought she ever could be.

'What a mess,' Julia said, and Sophie went over and put an arm around her.

'Don't be upset,' she said. 'It'll take her a long time to come round.'

'But in the meantime, what about us?' Julia said.

'We've got our lives, as she said. Let her pick up the pieces – she'll get over it in time. Isn't that what they say?'

'It's not just Daddy's dying,' Julia said. 'It's the—'

'Yes. Well,' Sophie stopped her short. 'I don't think she wants us around. She wants to grieve in peace.'

Julia nodded silently.

Sophie sighed. What a hell of a mess.

Seven

Vanessa Hastings had guests coming to lunch. The agents had made the suggestion, for as they explained, this contract was a very important one, and it was vital to bring it to a strong conclusion.

The guests turned out to be the managing director of Greensward, Daniel Green, who had made the offer for Heron Court, and Benjamin Green, his uncle, who was Sadie Thompson née Green's brother and a director of the company.

Edie Fisher had done the bedrooms and was making her way downstairs, passing the dining room, which was laid out for guests. On her way to the kitchen she saw the gleaming car – not that she knew it was a Ferrari, only that it was a conspicuous, super-looking car – and out of it stepped a man who looked slightly familiar, followed by another, taller man, and she thought they could have been relatives. Well, it was no business of hers. She didn't intend to stay here anyway. She had plenty of opportunities to work elsewhere.

There were bound to be plenty of visitors now that the house was under offer, which meant she would be out of a job. Mrs Hamlett had called her in to tell her the news, and said as long as she was required to work she could stay on. Temporarily, maybe, and she was not sure that she wanted to work in a retirement home – but then completion was a long way off, and it would be the decision of the development company. By the time all the plans had been drawn up, and from what she had gathered it was going to be quite a large development, months even years could go by.

Sadie had told her that Mrs Hastings had accepted the offer subject to planning permission which her son had made, and Sadie was very excited, for it meant that she could have an apartment in Heron Court, and an added bonus was that she would be near her friend, Edie Fisher.

Vanessa had spent the last two weeks seeing her accountants who were dealing with her bankruptcy, and she had held on to everything that she could, but there still seemed to be a lot of questions. Certain things, like her jewellery, were her own property, and she could keep her car, personal gifts which Stuart had made to her and bore statements to that effect were safe, but all in all, she was furious with the whole thing and blamed Stuart for his foolhardiness, but she quickly got down to the business in hand and intended to get as much out of the deal as she could – as she was entitled to, she told herself. Wearing what was her most expensive outfit but looking casually dressed, she would have made an impression on anyone, particularly a vulnerable male.

She was in the conservatory when they arrived. She had met Daniel Green several times, but the newcomer was a stranger. Taller than his nephew, with thick curling grey hair, dark eyes which held a twinkle although she could imagine the expression if things didn't go his way. She liked that in a man. Strength, particularly in a man, meant everything to Vanessa, who saw it as a challenge to herself. Stuart had been easy, he had never been a strong man, and the fact that he had died as he had, and left appalling debts, she saw as a sign of weakness. Vanessa had spent her life assessing men, and chose Stuart, for she could manipulate him, he would do whatever she asked, he would adore her. She also, in her own way, loved him, but the hardest thing to bear was that he had let her down, was a sham, a pretender, and she could hardly bear to admit to herself that she had made a mistake – been wrong. She had no intention of doing that a second time.

When Mrs Hamlett showed the two men in, she remained seated, holding out her hand in welcome. Her eyes were warm and welcoming, and both men, the younger and the older, were captivated by her beauty and charm.

'Benjamin Green,' the older man said as they shook hands.

Daniel saw her as an older woman. He had met her before and knew that she was not quite as perfect as she seemed, as hard as nails when it came to business, but Benjamin Green for all his experience of women, which was considerable, looked down into those eyes and felt a sense of drowning. He was not easily impressed. But this beauty, surrounded as she was by luxury in every sense of the word, nevertheless brought out in him the chivalry that he now realized he possessed. He wanted to protect her, take care of her. Despite her beauty, she looked fragile – to him, that beautiful mouth, the small straight nose, the warm brown eyes, and that cascade of dark hair – he found himself imagining her helpless, looking up at him with those great dark eyes. What a swine her husband must have been . . .

'Do sit down,' she urged them, in that low, melodious voice which was one of her greatest assets – the Englishness of it, Ben told himself, after the nasal speech of New Yorkers, was like a breath of fresh air.

While Mrs Hamlett waited for them to take their seats, Vanessa smiled at them across the table.

'I thought a drink might be acceptable before we have lunch, gentlemen, what do you say? We have something to celebrate, after all. What is your choice? I am sure we have something to please you – Mrs Hamlett? Wine, whisky, gin – martini – or beer, if you prefer, cold drinks—'

'Wine would be very nice,' they both said. 'Red wine,' and Mrs Hamlett left the room to return with a tray of wine glasses and three bottles, which she showed to Vanessa.

Vanessa looked at the labels. 'This one, I think – are you agreeable, gentlemen?' and she handed the bottle to Ben.

Looking at the chosen label, they both agreed.

'Fine, a good red,' Ben said. 'Allow me.'

'Thank you, sir,' and Mrs Hamlett left the room, while *he* opened the bottle and poured the three glasses and handed them round. There was a jug of iced water on the table, and two dishes of nuts and dry biscuits. Benjamin Green returned to the fray and raised his glass.

'I am very pleased to meet you, Mrs Hastings,' he said. 'I hope you are as happy as we are with the transaction – which I am told is going ahead smoothly both to our satisfaction and I hope yours.'

They raised their glasses, and Vanessa sat back, relaxing. A good-looking man, she told herself, with a clever man's charm, but she still held the whip hand until completion day, refusing to acknowledge that the money would not be hers. 'I imagine this will be quite a project – I'd like you to tell me something of your plans, since I am quite in the dark on these things.'

Daniel took over.

'Outline planning permission has been made to the council, but I have no doubt that we shall obtain full permission. The country is crying out for developments like this – with people living longer.'

'What does it entail – you must explain to me.'

'Briefly – this house will be the main centre – possibly four apartments within it, the dining room will be used as a communal dining room, the drawing room the same, the kitchen is certainly large enough in our opinion to deal with a number of residents' meals but we shall build on if we have to. Remember, each apartment will have a fully fitted kitchen, but there will always be some people who like to eat out. The main project will be the building of twenty-four apartments—'

'Goodness,' murmured Vanessa, 'quite an ambitious scheme.'

'We have built three such projects – one in Cheshire, one in Surrey and another in Hampshire – very successfully, but we think this one will be the most ambitious yet – it is such a beautiful setting.' And he raised his eyebrows to David, who nodded.

'You see, you have the advantage here of two and a half acres, and much can be done with that. Certainly a croquet lawn – and of course you already have a pool, I think probably tennis?' and he looked across at his uncle again, who nodded.

'Ten small cottages, there are always elderly people who prefer a house rather than an apartment – and if necessary we will build more later on – two-storey buildings, no higher than that.'

'I hadn't realized it was going to be such a large development,' Vanessa said, the thought crossing her mind that most of the villagers would oppose the plan when it came up, but it wasn't her problem what he did with it, and she certainly didn't care.

She was curious, though, about Benjamin Green.

'I understand you live and work in New York?' she said, giving him one of her most intimate smiles.

'Yes – I inherited a family business from my uncle – but since I am a director of my nephew's company, I have decided

to spend part of the year over here. After all, I was born here
– my roots are here.'

'I understand,' she murmured, and wondered if he was
married.

That the two men were wealthy men she was in no doubt,
and it might prove to be interesting. What age would Benjamin
be? Not sixty yet – while she was in her forties.

Stop daydreaming, Vanessa, she told herself. Find out more
about this business.

'And who do you expect to buy – or rent – these properties?'
she asked.

'They are to be sold, the apartments. People have to be over
sixty – and many people today appreciate this kind of living.
They have company, yet have their own accommodation, everything they could need is provided and they do not have to
mix with other people unless they want to.'

'But they have to pay for it,' she said, smiling.

'Of course,' and Daniel smiled too.

'And running a place like that costs,' she said. 'The overheads – the bills – must be tremendous.'

'And that is why they are quite expensive to buy.' Daniel
smiled wider.

'And are they?'

'Oh, yes,' he said. 'Nothing comes cheap.'

There was a tap on the door.

'Lunch is served,' Mrs Hamlett said.

Vanessa stood up.

'Gentlemen,' Vanessa said. 'Shall we go in?'

She took a deep breath. Today was Monday, and she would
put all thoughts of Wednesday out of her mind. For on
Wednesday, the receivers, the bailiffs, were coming – two
of them – but she wouldn't think about that. Bad enough to
have to sell her home to pay for Stuart's debts – but her
possessions, her private possessions! She would see about
that.

She beamed at the two men.

'This way,' she said, and led them into the dining room.

In Lady Somerville's garden, old Jim Pettisham was working in
the flower garden. It was his favourite part of the garden. In
his sailor cap, which was as old as the hills, his white hair,

what there was left, showing beneath it, he went from bed to bed, a rolling gait rather than a walk, his white beard and rosy face denoting a man born and bred in the country.

He loved this garden. Before his time someone had laid it out to perfection. The roses were going to be great this year, after the long cold winter, and everything was well on its way. The Judas tree; the mimosa, already in bloom; tulips; the daffodils almost finished, but not yet time to put in the bedding plants. That wouldn't be until May, and her Ladyship always left the choice to him, so that his visits to the nurseries were always an exciting affair. They knew him as an old, respected customer.

Today he was going to cut the front lawn, and although her Ladyship had offered him a sit-on mower, he wasn't having that. People would think he was past it, but there was plenty of life in him yet. As he passed the drawing-room windows he caught sight of her Ladyship sitting at her desk by the window. She was staring out into the garden and so engrossed in her thoughts, that he was sure she had not seen him.

Lady Somerville was indeed engrossed in her thoughts, for two weeks ago she had received a letter from the woman Graziella Massini – she had still not plucked up courage to call her 'granddaughter'.

The letter was quite creased where she had toyed with it, unfolding it, refolding it – and she still had not replied.

She opened it again for the umpteenth time – it was a pleasure to read such writing.

> *Dear Lady Somerville,*
>
> *Thank you for your kind letter.*
>
> *I hope you are well, and I look forward to meeting you. I intend to come to England at the end of May, and will be staying at the Clarendon Hotel, which I am assured is very comfortable. I shall be arriving late in the afternoon, and I enclose the card with the address and telephone number on it. I am due there on the 24th of May.*
>
> *I do hope you will agree to my paying you a visit, but of course that must be your decision. For my part, I am*

very excited at my proposed visit to England – it will be
my first – and I do hope you will feel it in your heart to
grant me a visit.
  Best wishes,
  Graziella Massini

Lady Somerville folded it again, and sat thinking as back and
forth across the lawn old Petty pushed the mower.

Finally, she took out a sheet of headed notepaper and began
her reply.

Dear Graziella Massini,
  Thank you for your letter.
  I hope you have a pleasant journey from Italy and
that you find the hotel comfortable.
  Please telephone me a few days after your arrival to
ensure my being here.
  Best wishes,
  Celia Somerville

What – and where else would she be? she wondered. This
was turning out to be a nonsense – and perhaps after all, she
would ignore it. But then the woman would write again – and
possibly again. What was the point of shelving it? Best get it
over and done with. She wrote the envelope and sealed it.
There, that was done. She would wait for Edie to come
tomorrow – although if the woman was coming, Mrs Baker
would be there to see her in – no, she would give it to Edie
to post – plenty of time for explanations later.

She pushed it under the blotter.

She had twenty-four hours to change her mind.

Laura Farrell was having a quick lunch with her friend Janet
Weatherall. Both women were in a state of suppressed excitement, for the building and decorating company had started
work this morning.

Laura had been there to see them in, and having made her
decisions clear to them after agreeing a price for the job, was
happy to leave the work to them. She would, she said, call in
at the end of most days to see how they were getting on or
answer any queries.

The cost of renovating was high, but she told herself that nothing these days was cheap, and there was no point in having a botched job. The biggest expense was the new kitchen, and she and Janet had spent the previous week choosing the fitments, and sorting out the flooring. The sale of her own house in Belford was going through, the young couple couldn't wait to move into it.

The large cubby hole in the hall on the way to the kitchen she had decided to turn into a shower cubicle, knowing that when Jamie came home from university he would be pleased with that. All in all, she made the most of what was available, and sat back to await events.

The change-of-user petition had gone through without any problem, which surprised her, and John Paynter, who had decided that there wasn't much he could do about it, helped smooth it through the council channels.

He could see the excitement in her eyes when she came in to see him, and all in all, decided that the poorer end of the High Street could do with a new look. He found himself growing curious as to what it would look like when finished, and was shocked to think about what it must be costing. How she would manage to run it was a different matter, and for the life of him he could not imagine how she was going to do it. Unlike most businesses, she would have to be out buying and delivering, working in the shop itself – altogether a daunting prospect for a young woman running it on her own.

Now, over a sandwich lunch, Janet and Laura were, as usual these days, discussing the running of the shop.

'I still think you should get in touch with Pat Mackay,' Janet said. 'She's a dab hand at buying and selling antiques, had a lot of experience.'

Laura frowned. 'Yes, I know her slightly, but I was hoping to do it on my own . . .'

Janet laid down her knife. 'Now that is ridiculous. When you are running that kind of shop you need all the help you can get – contacts, that's what it's all about.'

'I know – I am pig-headed,' Laura said.

'She's a "runner",' Janet said. 'You know, runs between antiques shops picking up things, selling them – she's always done it. She might have a title behind her, but she is brilliant.

I know, I caught up with her at several charity dos – she's great
– and brilliant with antiques. I suppose it's her background.'

'Yes, well – give me her phone number and I'll get in touch.
She could be useful, I suppose.'

'I should say,' Janet said, delving into her telephone book.
'Here you are.'

'Thanks,' Laura said, somewhat ungraciously.

'Well – what's the next step?'

'Nothing – I can't do anything except keep a check on what
the builders are doing.'

'When do you think you will open?'

'Three months' time, I hope. I have already been round to
the removal men to ask if they can move my stuff into the
shop – you'd be surprised how busy they are these days. I
also asked if they were prepared to move small items from
the shop to customers that I couldn't manage.'

'Oh, well done,' murmured Janet.

'But no – they were not, but put me in touch with someone
who is a small removal man, so when it gets nearer to the
time I will get in touch with him.'

'Getting exciting, isn't it?' Janet smiled. A lot of the excitement had rubbed off on her. Her days were so boring, she
was envious of Laura's.

'Come on,' Laura said. 'After we've cleared away, let's go
round to the shop, see how they are getting on.'

'But they only started this morning!' Janet cried.

'So?' Laura said. 'It's my shop, isn't it?'

Eight

On a fine morning in May, Graziella Massini left Rome airport, carrying her Louis Vuitton holdall, a further two cases being loaded to be taken to the hotel separately.

She had been very careful to pack the right clothes. As she saw it, Lady Somerville was a distinguished Englishwoman, and she packed her clothes with that in mind. Elegant, pure silk and cotton, although she couldn't imagine wearing it the weather being as it was supposed to be. Not too short – nor too long, come to that – wonderful scarves which in her opinion made each outfit what it was – elegant.

She was looked at, stared at, even in Rome, where beauty was of the first order, and many a male eye followed her progress through the booking hall to the embarkation area.

The flight was fairly short, and she changed planes at Heathrow for a taxi, which was to take her to Oxford.

She looked around her with interest at the drab houses fringing the outskirts, but it was a fine day and as they got farther out of London she could begin to see the charm of the English countryside.

For everywhere there were blossom trees, white and pink and red, while sheep grazed on the hills. It was like all the photographs she had seen of English life with here and there a patch of blue – English bluebells.

The driver drove through a few small towns and plenty of villages and gradually she warmed to the scene. It was as unlike Italy as it could possibly be.

When the spires of Oxford appeared, and the strange colour of the old buildings, the narrow streets, the people, carelessly dressed, the sheer beauty of the city, she was fascinated. When the driver pulled up outside the hotel and the doorman helped her with her luggage and then into the hotel, she really did begin to think that she was on the other side of the world.

So her father came from here – she could hardly believe it. It was all so strange.

After registering she was shown to a large, comfortable room and bathroom – it was in fact a suite – and to her joy, from the windows she could see the elegant towers and churches of Oxford. She was not easily moved, but the sight of her father's own domain brought tears to her eyes.

She kicked off her shoes and took off her jacket and lay on the bed in order to get her breath back after what seemed an earth-shattering experience. Glancing at her watch, she saw that it was eleven thirty – she had caught an early flight – and decided to take a shower and change. It was a very warm day, unusual for May, but she was not to know that and took her time, changing into a cotton dress, the ubiquitous narrow scarf around her neck, sandals – and went down to the bar for a drink before lunch.

She chose a cold drink – she would have wine with her lunch – then made her way to the dining room where she chose a salad and cheese. Eyes, particularly men's eyes, followed her wherever she went, but she was used to that, would have thought it odd if they didn't.

She had made no previous plans, but now she decided that she would take a taxi ride around the city with its colleges and spires – and her heart beat a little faster at the thought that she would drive out to Cedar Green – to get the layout, she told herself. Her imagination at home had been quite wild when she pictured it.

She had always thought Italy was the most beautiful country in the world, but this – this place was something else. The architecture, the buildings, the taxi driver pointed out the colleges to her and showed her most of the town. He took his time, for he was used to tourists' repeated questions. It was in the middle of the afternoon when he turned off towards the motorway, and she recalled the route by which she had arrived. He turned left at St Martin's Lane, and down the slight hill – it was gentle country, she thought, just as you imagine England might be. Turning in to Cedar Green he stopped the car.

'Well, this is it – Cedar Green. It's a small village.'

Her face softened. Her father had lived here and she could not have explained her emotions.

'Was there anywhere in particular you wanted to see?'

'Not really – from one end of the High Street to the other, I knew someone who lived here.'

'Oh – do you remember the address?'

'No – I am afraid I don't, but drive slowly and perhaps I will remember it.'

He turned past St Martin's Church, and she looked from right to left – mostly small shops – it was unlikely that the sort of house she had in mind was here. Still, the address was 'The Village' – and then she saw it.

With a wide frontage and lying back from the road, this beautiful white house, with pillars, long sash windows and magnificent urns full of flowers and a green lawns either side of the central path, and she gasped inwardly.

So that was it! She had not imagined anything so lovely. And how out of place – in this small High Street. It needed to be set in the countryside – but she wouldn't argue with that. It looked what it was: an expensive historical house, well kept – oh, she was sure now – this was her father's old home, and she swallowed hard.

'When you come to the end of the village, turn round and drive slowly past the High Street again. I think I have seen all I wanted to see.'

'Did you find the place you were looking for?'

'No – but I will come out here one day during my stay and look around.'

'Give us a ring,' he said. 'We are the best known taxi service in Oxford.'

'I am sure,' and she smiled back at him, her heart beating with excitement.

He wished all his lady clients looked like her.

Once back in her room, Graziella put down her handbag and slumped in the easy chair.

Well! What a beautiful house. And right in the middle of an English village. Her father's house. Yes – that is what it was. And her heart began to beat rapidly with excitement.

Tomorrow – but she wouldn't rush it – she would telephone her grandmother, Lady, she stressed – *Lady* Somerville – and she breathed deeply and closed her eyes.

Janie Paynter arrived home from school at May Tree Cottage. She always enjoyed going to her aunt's house, for it was likely that if her father was still at his office, and Edie was not there, she would find her own house empty.

'Auntie Barbara!' she called, and Barbara emerged from the kitchen, carrying a bouquet of flowers which she stood in a vase in the hall.

'Darling! How did you get on today?'

'Fine – Miss Webster was in a good mood for once.'

She eased the satchel of books off her shoulder and hung it in the cloakroom, washing her hands – something her aunt always insisted on.

Coming back, she followed Barbara to the kitchen sink.

'When Mummy died – do you think she went to heaven?'

Oh, God! And Barbara thought, not for the first time, how wonderful it would be if John could find a new wife who would help her with these problems. Janie needed a mother, and if there was one thing Barbara hated it was planting her own beliefs into the girl's head, but she refused to tell lies. Time would come, perhaps soon, when Janie would cease to ask these questions on religious topics – after all, she must discuss them at school, but obviously wanted an older person's opinion.

She stood and faced her. Such a pretty little thing, Janie. Thin, but she had never been plump, she was like her mother. Fair skinned, fair haired – an ethereal look about her.

'What do *you* think?' she countered.

'I dunno,' Janie said. 'I'd like to think so, but it – well, it's not practical, is it? I mean, where are all the dead people? Floating around?'

'Their souls are, I expect.'

'You mean, like dust particles everywhere?'

Barbara permitted herself a smile. 'No – not really. I think – I believe – that if you have had children, then you leave your genes. That has been proven, hasn't it?'

'So I might have some of Mummy's genes?'

'And Daddy's,' Barbara said.

'And if you don't have children – that's it? That's the lot?'

Barbara shrugged and decided to tell her niece what had been on her mind all day. 'Listen, Janie, I've been thinking—'

'About life after death?' Janie asked brightly.

'No – something quite different, and I wonder what you think of the idea. I have decided to give a garden party—' and she waited for the news to sink in.

'Auntie Barbara!' She threw her arms around Barbara's neck.
'Really? When?'

'Sometime next month.'

'Oh, great! Where? Here?'

'No – in your garden – your father's garden. I have organized
plenty of garden parties and fetes for charities, usually in
the village hall garden, but why not in your garden? It'll be
for our friends – and relatives. You can help me organize it.'

Janie's blue eyes were sparkling. 'Oh, what a lovely idea!
Who will you ask?'

'Well, now that will need going into. After all, we know
lots of people – and if it's a fine day, it will be lovely in your
garden. Of course, your daddy will have to agree—'

'Oh, he'll love it!' Janie cried. 'When do you think – which
day?'

'A Saturday at the end of June, so we haven't given ourselves
much time, but if we get cracking – say the last Saturday in
June – get the invitations out – after all, people go away in
July – and I thought it would be a good time, although it is
not giving them much notice.'

Janie was jumping about in excitement. Poor little thing,
thought Barbara – why did I never think of it before? I shall
have to get busy, sort out a list of invitations.

'Who will you ask?'

'Well, you will have to help me – neighbours, some of your
daddy's clients,' and Janie's face fell.

'Not business people.'

'No – you leave it to me. After all, I have heaps of friends
in the village – and you might like to ask a few friends yourself. In fact, we shall have to get cracking right away – there
is not a lot of time – we are in to the fourth week of May.
So, invitation cards – you can help me with those.'

Janie hugged her. 'Will we have music?'

Barbara looked doubtful. 'Well, music of some kind – don't
forget, we have to supply all the food and so on. Perhaps it
would be better to get caterers in.'

'No, we can manage,' Janie assured her. 'We'll have tables
filled with this and that – we could have a barbecue.'

'But that makes a lot of work for your daddy, and I don't
think he would like that, unless we got people in – no, let's
start with an afternoon garden party – quite literally tea in the

garden. After all, your daddy's garden is perfect for that. Edie
will be around, I hope – and there is no one like Edie for
giving a hand.'

Janie's eyes were shining.

'Tell you what – have you got much homework?'

'No, not a lot.'

'Well, do it now, then you can help me with a list of names.'

But Janie had already gone to get her satchel.

The following day, Graziella wrote to her grandmother. She
had decided not to telephone her, since answering the phone
and being confronted suddenly with an unknown voice might
make Lady Somerville uncomfortable.

She used hotel notepaper, and made the message brief.

> *Dear Lady Somerville,*
>
> *I arrived at the above hotel yesterday, and very
> comfortable it is. I had a good flight from Rome and a
> very pleasurable journey to Oxford.*
>
> *Now that I am here, I would be delighted if I could
> visit you and make your acquaintance.*
>
> *I shall be here for a week and hope this will be
> convenient for you.*
>
> *Best wishes,*
> *Graziella Massini*

She reread the letter, and finding no fault with it addressed it
to Lady Somerville in Cedar Green.

There – and she took it down to the receptionist for it to
be posted.

John Paynter was sitting at his desk at home when a tap came
on the door, and his sister Barbara entered.

He looked up. 'Oh, Barbara – everything all right?'

'Are you busy?'

Always the first question to John.

'Nothing that can't wait,' and he sat back in his chair.

She dragged up a chair and sat opposite him. 'John, I've
had an idea.'

'Oh, Lord,' said in mock horror.

'No, seriously – why don't we give a garden party? In June?'

'Who's "we"?' he asked.

'Well, I would arrange it all, but if we could have it in your garden . . .'

'*My* garden? What's this all about?' He looked genuinely puzzled.

'Well, to start with yours is a lovely garden – and secondly I thought it might be nice for young Janie.'

'Oh.' He looked relieved. 'You mean a young people's party.'

'No, I don't, John. I mean for friends, neighbours – she could invite some friends of her own.'

'Who is going to organize this?'

'Well, I am – with Janie's help,' and he looked so apprehensive she felt sorry for him. His life had been deadly dull since Lyn died. Still, that's what it was all about – a gathering, a village do.

'I would have thought you had enough to do, organizing your village charities.'

'This is a personal thing. Oh, go on, John, think about it.'

'How many?'

'I have no idea – yet. Janie is delighted to help me, and there will be Edie and other people to give a hand.'

'Well,' he seemed doubtful. 'There's an awful lot of work involved . . .'

'You sound like a real old misery,' she said.

'Well, you come in and shock me with your ideas – and then there's the garden – I don't want everyone tramping down the—'

'More important than people, eh, John?' Now she was cross.

'Whose idea was this?' he asked suspiciously.

'Mine,' she said, standing up. 'Think about it, John – if you are really against it, then so be it – but I am keen – and so is Janie. We only need your backing.'

'Look, let me think about it – I see what you're getting at. She meets precious few people socially . . .'

She grabbed at this.

'That's what I mean, John. Let me get a few figures out and ideas – and I'll let you know.' She made her way out. 'After all, some of your personal friends – some of the shopkeepers—'

'I see – like a Rotary Club do?'

'No,' and she laughed. 'But they are a decent lot most of them – some of them.'

'Well, you should know,' he said, but he was smiling.

Halfway there, Barbara thought happily. When Edie came tomorrow she would ask her if she was free on that last Saturday in June and she and Janie would make a list – oh, not too many – but enough to make a jolly crowd. And Annie Winsome – with her cooking and baking – she would only be too pleased to cook some cakes and things – and Mattie Ransome with her famous thin sandwiches – oh, yes, she could see it coming off – how exciting – they could borrow the tea urn from the Women's Union.

But deep down and at the back of her mind was the thought that if John could meet some nice women socially . . .

You're like the matchmaker in *Fiddler on the Roof*, she thought. Seriously, he should have more of a social life, instead of being cooped up in that office dealing with business matters – and mostly of a personal nature.

And whilst no good came of interfering, nevertheless, surely a garden party could do no harm.

If the Queen could hold a garden party, why couldn't she?

Two days later, Graziella Massini received a letter from Lady Somerville.

> *Please come to lunch on Friday the twenty-fifth of May at twelve thirty. If this is not convenient perhaps you would telephone Mrs Baker, my housekeeper.*

Graziella sat thinking. So far so good.

Nine

In her hotel room, Graziella Massini sat brushing her luxuriant hair, her lovely eyes twinkling back at her with concealed excitement. For she was excited. Nothing fazed Graziella – but she guessed the old lady might be a bit het up.

Well – she had been officially invited, and the taxi would be here soon.

She swept the hair off her face, guessing that an elderly lady would not wish to see her hair all over her face. She was appalled at how many English girls just let it hang with no effort made to dress it, but that wasn't her way. She was fussy down to the last toenail, and looked down at them now, their natural polish just shining through her pure silk tights.

Now for the outfit.

It was a warm day – she hadn't expected it to be this kind of weather so early in the year – but fortunately she had brought enough to deal with any kind of weather or situation. Her cream linen skirt lay on the bed – she couldn't go wrong in that – and a black and cream silk jersey top – Gucci – and over that the short tailored cream jacket. With it she would wear her black jet beads and her small black Dior handbag.

Make-up she applied carefully – there was nothing she did not know about make-up – like most Italian women except that she had had the advantage of being the daughter of an actress – and there was nothing her mother did not know about that.

High heels – but not too high; she had no wish to offend the old lady – her *grandmother*, she kept reminding herself, and taking a good look at her back view in the long mirror, sat herself down to await the call from reception that the taxi had arrived.

Her heart was beating a little faster when it finally came,

and she was pleased to see that it was the same driver who had driven her before.

She greeted him, and as for him, he thought he had never seen such a stunning-looking woman.

'Good morning, Madam – Cedar Green, is it?'

'Yes. I have the address now,' and she smiled at him. 'The White House.'

'Know it well – by sight,' he said. 'One of the finest houses in the neighbourhood.'

You could say that again, thought Graziella, and sat back to enjoy the short journey.

The taxi pulled into the short drive of The White House, and stopped outside the front door. Graziella paid the driver and said she would give him a ring when she wanted to return to the hotel, and head held high, rang the impressive brass bell.

If Mrs Baker was surprised to see her, she hid it well. She had not expected anyone in the least like this. The woman had a delightful smile, and Mrs Baker was not the first person to be impressed.

It was exactly twelve thirty when she opened the door wide to allow the visitor in.

'Good afternoon, Mrs—?'

'Graziella Massini – Lady Somerville is expecting me.'

Mrs Baker closed the door and led the way through to the drawing room.

'Your visitor, milady,' she said, and as Graziella entered the room, closed the door behind her, hurrying into the kitchen to get over the surprise of seeing someone like this young woman in The White House.

Lady Somerville, sitting upright in her high-backed chair, saw with a shock the beautiful young woman in the cream suit, and her first thought was of her son David, for despite her dark feminine beauty, she was the image of him. She felt a lump rise in her throat – she had not expected this – and the young woman walked towards her.

'Please sit down,' Lady Somerville said, leaving Graziella to choose her own seat. She made no effort to shake her hand or greet her in any way, but could hardly take her eyes off her, the likeness to David was so apparent. David had been dark with dark eyes and brows, but there was something about the shape of the mouth, the way the girl looked at her straight and unflinching, she almost felt like weeping, except that she was not by nature an emotional woman.

Graziella put her handbag down by her side and removed her gloves.

'Are you well, Lady Somerville? I hope this is not too much of an ordeal for you.'

'Not at all,' and her voice didn't sound as it usually did. The young woman had a low-pitched voice, with the slightest accent, most attractive she decided, but she needed time to pull herself together, almost wishing now that she had not agreed to the meeting.

'What a beautiful room,' Graziella said, looking around.

'But then it is a beautiful house.'

'It belonged to my husband's family,' Lady Somerville said, then, mindful of the fact that she was the hostess, decided the time had come for questions.

'So this is your first visit to England?' she said.

'Yes – although I have always longed to come here,' Graziella said. 'My father talked about it often – that is, before—'

'He died,' Lady Somerville said.

Graziella was an actress if she was nothing else, and lowered her eyes at the sadness of it. But this she genuinely felt – sometimes she thought that she would never get over it.

'He was a wonderful man,' she said, looking straight into Lady Somerville's faded eyes, 'and a wonderful father.'

'I am sure,' Lady Somerville said, and now had difficulty keeping back the tears, for the young woman looked so much like him. His expressions, his way of talking – even though she had a slight accent and David spoke impeccable English.

'Tell me about your life – in Rome, is it? Is that where you are living now?'

'Yes, ever since Father died,' Graziella said. 'Although after he died we moved to an apartment – and when I . . .' she hesitated.

'You are married?' Lady Somerville asked.

'Oh, no!' Graziella whispered. 'Although I was, for a time but . . . I moved back into Mama's apartment when—'

Lady Somerville was not going to probe and waited for the explanation to be forthcoming. She inclined her head slightly, indicating that she wished Graziella to go on.

'I was married briefly – to an Italian count – but—' she looked down, then took out a lacy handkerchief from her handbag. 'Excuse me, Lady Somerville,' she whispered. The old lady was silent, she did not intend to give her any help. Graziella soon sensed the mood of her grandmother, and replacing her handkerchief in her handbag, sat up straight, as though ready for any further questions.

'The marriage did not last?' Lady Somerville said.

'No – unfortunately,' Graziella said, in command again now. 'I was young and got carried away – despite Mama's protestations.' She didn't say her mother had been enthusiastic about the marriage. 'He was a handsome man—'

And a count and wealthy, Lady Somerville decided. 'So?' she urged her on.

'But when I discovered that he had been unfaithful – that was the end of it.' And she looked straight into Lady Somerville's eyes, her deep brown eyes wide and innocent as a child.

'That is very sad,' Lady Somerville said. 'So you moved back into your mother's apartment.'

'After she died – sadly,' Graziella said. 'She was too young to die.'

But her Ladyship was not giving out sympathy that day, and when Mrs Baker tapped on the door to tell them lunch would be in five minutes, she stood up, and leaning heavily on her stick, walked over to the window.

Then she turned.

'I think I shall have to call you Graziella – so will you escort me into lunch, Graziella?'

'With pleasure,' Graziella said, and the two of them went into the dining room.

Not missing a trick, Graziella swiftly observed the beautiful gardens seen through the large French windows, the flower displays and the trees, and not to be understated, the furniture, which was almost all French and exquisite, as were the silk curtains.

She assisted her Ladyship when it came to sitting down, and made sure her napkin was unfolded and on her lap – a fact which did not go unnoticed by Lady Somerville. When Mrs Baker served the cold consommé Graziella was aware of tension and perhaps disapproval on Mrs Baker's part – but she was not surprised, deeming it a kind of jealousy.

The lunch of salmon and salad was delicious, and she made a point of saying so in front of Mrs Baker. There were raspberries and cream to follow and afterwards coffee in the drawing room.

By now, Lady Somerville was more relaxed, particularly as Graziella put herself out to be a help in any way she could without losing any of her dignity.

'You are happy in the hotel?' she asked.

'Oh, yes, very much so,' Graziella said. 'I have booked until the weekend, then I must get back and finish off the personal business I have had to deal with since Mama died.'

'It was not long ago, then?' Lady Somerville said.

'Just a few weeks,' Graziella said sadly. 'And there has been so much clearing up to do – Mama was not a good businesswoman,' and she smiled ruefully. 'It was while I was going through her papers that I found your name and address – and of course many of my father's personal papers.'

Lady Somerville's curiosity was aroused, but she said nothing. What else might there be among David's papers?

'And what will you do with your life now?' she asked.

Graziella gave a deep sigh.

'Well, I am on my own now – so I shall have to plan what to do with the rest of my life. I will not stay on in the flat, I do know that. So many memories.'

And the dark lashes lay on her cheeks.

She was really beautiful, Lady Somerville thought – a granddaughter to be proud of. And so like David – she brought him back more than anything else could.

After Mrs Baker had taken away the coffee cups, Graziella made a move to go.

'You are not leaving yet?' Lady Somerville said.

'Yes,' and Graziella gave her a beautiful smile. 'I must not tire you out and I expect you are ready for a little rest. It has been very exhausting for you. Are you feeling well? Is there anything I can do for you?'

What a nice girl! Lady Somerville thought. I will almost be sorry to see her go. The place will seem empty somehow.

'Would you mind if I made a call to the taxi company? Perhaps Mrs Baker will do it for me – I have the number here—' and she extracted a card from her handbag.

'Of course, my dear,' Lady Somerville said, and rang the bell on her desk for Mrs Baker.

When Mrs Baker disappeared, Graziella went over to the window, and surveyed the front garden with the high iron gates leading to the village.

'What a lovely village!' she said. 'Everything I ever imagined of an English village.'

'You must come again,' said Lady Somerville, surprising herself. She would be sorry to see her go. After all, she was her – yes, her only relative, well, her only close relative.

Then the taxi arrived, and Lady Somerville escorted Graziella to the front door, where she took her hand.

'Goodbye, my dear, and I hope we meet again.'

'Thank you,' Graziella said, and swiftly bent and gave a light kiss to the fair wrinkled cheek.

'Thank you – and goodbye.'

Once in the taxi looking back, Graziella caught sight of Mrs Baker's disapproving eye. Too bad, she thought. Well – that was worth doing.

Ten

L aura Grey and Janet Weatherall went to inspect the work being done on Laura's new venture.

It was early June and work on the antiques shop was well under way. The whole premises had been emptied and cleared and the new kitchen which Laura and Janet had gone to so much trouble to plan, was almost fitted and finished. It was small after her previous kitchen, but she considered it ample for her needs. After all, she was there on her own most of the time, only when Jamie came home would there be the two of them. The walls had been stripped, the new fitments put in, a new tiled floor laid, and there was space for a washing machine and a dishwasher. Janet privately kept her thoughts to herself – she could not imagine living in such poky surround-ings – but in spite of her misgivings, she was quite excited at the project of the shop itself.

The shower room went in next, and although upstairs there was a bathroom, Laura decided she would manage with the old suite and promised herself a new white bathroom if and when she had enough money to do so.

Then came the restoration of the shop itself, stripped and painted a dark red colour which Laura decided was a perfect background for antiques, while the small garden shed came into its own for keeping the workmen's tools and materials to hand.

During this time Jamie came home one weekend from college for the first time, and seemed to recognize what his mother was up to. Before that he had thought it was all a figment of her imagination, a kind of wishful thinking.

But he had to hand it to her. He was intrigued, while doubtful of its success, but he wouldn't say anything to his mother of his doubts. He was glad to see she had a new interest – heaven knew she deserved it after the life she had lived with his father.

He had adored his father, only as he grew older did he realize what his mother had to endure with regard to his father's womanising. His father was a handsome man and he adored women – and Jamie wasn't slow to realize that women were attracted to him, and there were many opportunities for him to be unfaithful. When the divorce came Jamie was devastated but realized that things could not go on as they were. It wasn't fair on his mother, whom he adored.

So now, having a life of his own, he was only too pleased to see that she had another interest to keep her busy, for he sensed that she was not only a good mother, but a nice woman, with a sense of humour, and after all, that counted for everything.

He was intrigued by the whole set-up and while he could not imagine how she was going to do it, nevertheless gave her a hand when she needed it, and Laura was more than grateful for his acceptance of the situation.

On the Friday morning while he was at the shop, the doorbell rang, and he answered it to find a friendly woman there who looked vaguely familiar.

'Hallo – are you Jamie?' she asked.

'Yes.'

'I'm Barbara – Barbara Faulkner, a friend of your mother's. Is she in?'

'Yes, she is,' he said, turning and calling out to her.

Laura appeared from the back of the house. 'Oh, Barbara – how nice to see you.'

'I won't interrupt you – I can see you are awfully busy.'

Laura turned. 'You've met Mrs Faulkner – my son, Jamie.'

'Yes,' and they shook hands.

'Come in – see how we are getting on.'

She led the way. 'Janet is here – Janet Weatherall.'

Through the newly painted shop and then into the kitchen.

'Hallo, Janet – shouldn't interrupt you, you must be so busy.'

'Oh – we can spare a moment,' Laura said. 'I'd ask you to sit down but there aren't any chairs yet,' and she laughed.

'I won't keep you – I just wanted to ask you to tea,' and she waited for the words to sink in.

Laura frowned.

'Excuse me,' and Jamie disappeared into the garden.

'To tea?'

'Well, I don't quite mean that, but we are having a sort of garden party – in June – at my brother's house – John Paynter – you know him, don't you?'

'Of course, he is my solicitor.'

'Well, we are giving a garden party – and to tell the truth, we need an excuse so we decided it would be to wish you good luck in your new venture,' and Laura stared at her. 'It's on Saturday the thirtieth of June.'

'What?'

'I know – mad, isn't it? – but would you come, as guest of honour? If not, we'll make it another day.'

'I hope to open the following Monday – the second of July.'

'What do you think?'

'I think it's a lovely idea, and I would love to come – if I can spare the time,' she added doubtfully.

'Well, once the shop is open you won't have much time for frivolous things.'

'True.'

'Go on – say you'll come – you deserve a break,' Janet said, 'and there is nothing like a send off.' She turned to Janet. 'And you are invited too – and your husband – I will be sending you an invitation.'

'How lovely!' Janet said, and she meant it.

'Jamie, too, if he'd like to come – there will be a few young people there.'

'Do you do this every year?' Laura asked.

'No, it is my first effort – but if it's a success then we certainly will, so I can count you in then?'

'Yes, thank you.'

'Well, I'll be off then – good luck. I'll let myself out,' Barbara said, and she was gone.

'Well!' Janet said. 'What was all that about?'

'No idea – but isn't it nice of her?'

'Yes, and to ask me too. I didn't say anything, but George will be away that weekend.'

'Never mind – you will be there – but you know, really, Jan, it's an awkward time – just before the opening of the shop . . .'

'Well, you won't get any time *after* it's open.'

'I know, but I imagined that everything would be moved

in on the Saturday, although I haven't booked and I should have done . . .'

'So get on to the removal people straight away and ask them to make it Friday, then you will have Saturday morning to see to it, and Sunday – I'll give you a hand, George will be away all week.'

'Oh, you are a good soul – but you will agree, it is an awkward time to pick.'

'Only if you make it so. Work around it. If they deliver the goods on Friday, it's only a question of putting the furniture in situ and hanging pictures and things, isn't it?'

Laura looked worried. 'That's what I mean.'

'Well, you can work behind the scenes during the previous week, then that just leaves the delivery of the furniture, doesn't it? Then heighho, come Monday, pull back the curtains—'

'I'm not having curtains – blinds.'

'So pull up the blinds, and there we have it – a new antiques shop, and crowds waiting to come in.'

'Oh, don't, Janet – I'm getting cold feet.'

'No you're not, you're just fazed because you've been asked to a tea party,' and suddenly they both had a fit of the giggles.

'Now come on,' Janet said. 'Are we going round to your house to look at what you've got upstairs? I can't wait.'

'Yes, let's go,' Laura said.

When they arrived in Belford, they drove through the village and into a side avenue which was lined with blossom trees, finished now, but in full leaf. Laura's house was on the left-hand side, an imposing residence with a 'Sale Agreed' board up outside.

'That must give you a good feeling,' Janet said.

Laura grinned. 'It does – but I shall be glad when the move is over.'

She unlocked the door and they went into the house.

'Cup of tea?'

'No thanks – I can't wait to see the stuff.'

'Then follow me.'

The house had a third floor, two attic rooms, in most of the houses used as a games room or spare bedrooms. Once they reached the top, Laura unlocked the door. It was dark inside, for the curtains were drawn and blinds down.

'I have to do this to keep out the sun, which would bleach

the furniture although as you can see I have dust covers over everything.'

The walls were lined with pictures, most of which were covered by sheets, as was everything else in the room, while from the ceiling hung three chandeliers also draped with covers. Laura swept back one of the covers to expose a French boule cabinet.

'Ooh,' Janet breathed. 'Is it all like this?'

'It's mostly English, actually,' Laura said, smiling. 'My parents had some lovely things – my father was a collector. I refused to sell it when they died – and I am pleased now that I didn't.'

'You were very wise. Is it all right? No damage?'

'Not as far as I can see.'

'You know, Laura, if you had put this stuff into auction it would have fetched a bomb.'

'Yes, I know that – but, well, I wanted to do something on my own, and this seemed to be the answer.'

I hope you're right, thought Janet.

Laura took another cover off to expose a walnut commode.

'Eighteenth century – Italian,' Laura said.

'Is everything as lovely as this?' Janet asked.

'Yes,' she said, and grinned. 'As far as I am concerned.'

'And do you really know about pricing it – that's the hardest part, isn't it?'

'Yes, I suppose – but I have always kept up with prices and I have excellent up to date price guides.'

'I had no idea you were so knowledgeable!' Janet said. 'And all this to be moved out.'

'Yes – everything up here.'

'Jamie not interested?'

'No, never has been – I have a few bits of my own which I am keeping which will stay with me in the new place – otherwise, it's all for sale.'

'Bit of a wrench,' Janet said.

'In a way, but I've lived with it ever since I can remember and it is getting to be a bit of a worry – anyway we shall see,' she said, closing the door behind them.

She had some pluck, Janet thought.

'I'll drive you back now,' Laura said. 'Perhaps we could have some lunch on the way – have you time?'

'Yes – why not?'
And in fine fettle the two women made for Cedar Green.

Lady Somerville had to admit that after Graziella's visit she
had felt drained, drained but exhilarated. Excited too, at the
thought that this young woman was her own granddaughter,
her own son's child. It took some believing, and it was hard
to accept now that she had delayed the decision to meet.

But it was done now, and she admitted to herself that she
could not wait to see her again.

Youth, she thought, and beauty – it uplifted the soul.

No further promises had been made about a further visit,
but she could remedy that. A telephone call to the hotel, even,
but she would sleep on it. She must not rush into things.

When Mrs Baker brought her bedtime drink, she pulled the
curtains and folded the coverlet back.

'Did you enjoy your luncheon, milady?' she asked, that
being the farthest she dare go to mention the unusual visitor.

'Yes, it was excellent – we enjoyed it very much. Such a
joy to have her visit me – my son's only child, you know –
lives in Italy.'

'Oh.' There seemed to be no answer to that, although Mrs
Baker was more than curious. 'A very beautiful young lady,
if I may so,' she offered.

'Yes, she is, and so like my son – I have not seen her for
years,' which she thought took care of the situation.

More questions would have seemed impertinent, so Mrs
Baker wished her goodnight and closed the door softly behind
her.

Well! A relative. She had had no idea her Ladyship had
any relatives, and wondered if they might be seeing her again.

Lady Somerville pondered the situation over her bedtime
drink. Of course, she wanted to see her again – and made up
her mind to write to Graziella the very next day. Telephone
calls could be listened to by all sorts of undesirables, and she
would write – a personal letter.

The next day seated at her desk, she composed a further letter.

Dear Graziella,
  *I so enjoyed your visit yesterday, and was set to wonder
how long you would be staying in England? It occurred*

to me that you might like to spend a few days with me – we have such a lot to talk about.

Perhaps you would let me know your movements so that I can arrange something convenient for both of us?

Best wishes,

Celia Somerville

On receiving this, Graziella took some time replying. She was not going to show how keen she was for a further invitation.

Over the next few days, which she spent touring the Oxfordshire countryside and enjoying herself immensely, she composed her letter, deciding to take the bull by the horns and call her grandmother by her correct name.

Dear Grandmother,

How very nice to hear from you. I have been touring the beautiful Oxfordshire countryside, and have quite fallen in love with it.

Thank you for your kind invitation. Unfortunately I have to return to Rome to deal with several business matters which have arisen, and I will not be returning to England until the last week in June. Could we arrange something after that date? I shall be returning on the 27th of June, and will stay at the same hotel.

I do hope this time will be convenient to you, and I await to hear from you.

Please stay well.

Affectionately,

Graziella

This letter created a great deal of excitement for Lady Somerville, and she answered it at once.

My dear Graziella,

Please come straight here to stay at The White House. I look forward to seeing you again.

Have a safe journey.

Best wishes,

Your affectionate grandmother

Graziella hugged the letter to her when it arrived, and did a little twirl. There! You see – it had all been worthwhile. She must let her know the exact date and time of her arrival. Oh – she couldn't wait

Back at Churchgate House, Barbara and Janie were going over the final list of people to ask for the great day. The list had grown longer since they had started and Barbara was about to have it printed. The date fixed was for June the thirtieth, a Saturday, and they prayed that the weather would be fine.

'I'm getting quite excited, Auntie Barbara,' Janie said.

'Well, there will be lots to do,' Barbara said. 'Thank goodness for Edie – and now for the orders for the cakes and things.'

Janie's eyes shone.

She couldn't wait.

Eleven

John Paynter looked hard at the list in front of him, frowning as he did so, for he was only going along with the idea of the garden party for his sister's and his daughter's sake.

'OK,' he said, handing it back to her. 'But I don't think Green, the developer—'

'Oh, John, why not? His sister Sadie is coming, she is a friend of Edie's.'

'What's that got to do with it?'

'Well, I just thought since he is going to be a resident he might like to meet the village people.'

'Resident be damned! He is going to develop Heron Court – and then we won't see him for dust!'

She dug in her heels. 'Well, I think it is a good idea, could be interesting. Still, as you say, it really doesn't matter.' After all, he had given his permission for the event, which had surprised her in the first place.

'Oh, well, as Janie would say, go on then,' he said. 'How is it all coming along?'

'The next thing is to deliver the cards. Janie and I will do that.'

'All set on the eats front? What time does it start?'

'Four o'clock – and I was wondering what you thought about a glass of champagne at the end of the day?'

'Good God, Barbara! How long is it going on for?'

' 'Til it finishes,' she said, digging her heels in. 'I must fly – thanks for the coffee!' And she was gone.

He was already regretting it. One of her madcap ideas. Women!

On the last week in June, it was arranged that the furniture and pictures from Laura's home for the gallery would be collected by the removal people on the Thursday preceding the tea party. This was to ensure that plenty of time was given to arranging things, and Janet Weatherall was to give a hand.

She helped Laura to carry the small pictures and lamps and boxes of vases, making two journeys back to Cedar Green, where they busied themselves hanging pictures where Laura thought suitable until the removal men arrived.

Already it was beginning to take shape and the more pictures Laura put up, the more it looked like a possible gallery.

She had bought a little van for the buying and delivering of small pieces of furniture, while the man recommended by the removal men said he was only too glad to help with the larger pieces. Her own small car was still in the garage in Belford, mainly for Jamie's use when he came home, and she hoped to find a garage somewhere in Cedar Green for it, since her small van was needed to be near the shop.

When the van arrived and the two shop doors opened wide you could see the possibilities of an interesting little gallery. The first thing was a small desk, which was for Laura's own use, and then came the finer things.

As far as she could she asked the men to place things in situ, and surprisingly the small shop took everything, even if it did look a bit crowded. The dark red walls made a perfect background and Janet saw Laura's eyes sparkling with excitement. Electricians had been the day before to hang the chandeliers, all of which bore a price tag, and when lit the shop looked most impressive. Smaller pieces were stacked in the narrow hallway until they could be placed.

In each window the men placed the most interesting of the pieces of furniture, the Sheraton walnut commode and the French Louis XV desk in tulipwood and kingswood, two standard lamps, and a pair of oak wheel-back chairs, a mahogany plant stand behind them and on the far wall was to hang a bookcase with a table in the centre and various small items dotted about in the spaces.

'Now for the final trip back to Belford – for the small things, the vases and pots and things. I said I would take them in the van. By the time Monday comes round with the flowers and plants and everything I think it will look rather nice.'

She stood back by the door and surveyed it all, her eyes shining.

'Wonderful!' Janet said, as the removal men packed up their boxes and heavy covers, preparing to leave.

'I am delighted that Edie is free on Friday afternoon to come and polish everything. She will be a boon, that woman.'

'Yes, for don't forget she has got the tea party on Saturday and we don't want to tire her out.'

'Well, I shall do some this evening,' Laura said.

'You're coming back with me for a meal,' Janet said. 'George is still in New York.'

'That would be nice,' Laura said gratefully. It was good to have a friend like Janet. 'I have another week at Belford, before I actually move out. Jamie will be home that weekend to give me a hand. And the people buying it want to move in as soon as possible, so it should all be over and done with next weekend – and imagine, I shall have had the gallery a week!'

'Oh, I do wish you well,' Janet said, and sighed. 'After we've had a meal, why don't you stay the night, save driving back to Belford? Then you'd be on the spot in the morning to check everything at the shop.'

'Oh, could I? I must say it's been quite a day, I should appreciate that.'

'I thought those solid brass candlesticks looked nice on the table,' Janet said. 'But you are short of silver, aren't you?'

'Yes, my weakest link,' Laura said.

'Why is that?'

'Well, I worked with a girl at Sotheby's for a spell and she told me about silver – it was her speciality – and I realized how little I knew about it. Also she explained how it was easy to eradicate marks underneath and put new ones on – in fact it left me feeling so unsure that I didn't think I wanted to know. So I've always kept away from silver.'

'But it looks nice in an antiques shop, and that's where Pat Mackay would come in – she's a dab hand at silver.'

Laura smiled to herself. Janet seemed quite determined to get Pat into the business somehow. Well, perhaps she would.

Outside the shop, still with its blinds down, they looked at the impression it made to outsiders, with its new green paint and over the door in the centre of the two windows, an oval nameplate in grey bordered with gold. 'Laura Grey' – yes, very impressive.

Both women had a shower when they arrived at Janet's house in Cedar Green, and after the muddles of both her properties, Laura was still surprised at the standards Janet kept in her house. Everywhere was immaculate, polished, and shining, not a thing out of place, the room that she had freshly aired with fresh curtains and bedding, a vase of flowers on the dressing table – did Janet keep this up all the time?

In a borrowed dressing gown, she and Janet sat having a glass of wine in the kitchen. She was a good cook, Janet, and always kept her large fridge well stocked in case of visitors and George's business associates.

It was good to relax, waiting for an excellent meal of chicken casserole – Janet was such a good organizer.

They talked over the meal of the forthcoming tea party, and who might be going until the dishes were put in the dishwasher and everything cleared away.

The phone rang around nine thirty and Janet answered it.

'George! Where are you?'

Laura got up and made ready to go up to bed.

'It's George,' Janet whispered, 'he's at Heathrow.'

'Oh,' Laura said, wishing she hadn't agreed to stay overnight. That meant he would be home shortly. She had no liking for George Weatherall.

Janet put the phone down looking puzzled.

'He will be home in an hour or so,' she said. 'I wonder why he changed his plans?'

'I'm going up – if that's all right with you,' Laura said, giving her friend a swift kiss. 'Anything else I can do?'

'No, sweetie, that's fine. Get a good night's rest – you're going to need it. You know where everything is . . .' but Laura could see by her eyes that her thoughts were elsewhere.

'Goodnight, then – and thank you.'

'My pleasure,' Janet said. 'Get up when you feel like it, except you probably want to make an early start.'

'Yes, that's for sure,' Laura said, and laughed and went on her way up to bed.

Ninety minutes after he had telephoned, the key to the front door turned and George Weatherall was inside. Waiting for him in the hall was Janet, who leaned forward to kiss him, but he brushed her aside. Instantly she could sense his mood. Presumably his luggage was still in the car.

'Everything all right?' she asked him, but he didn't look at her, instead went straight into the kitchen. She followed him, closing the door behind her.

'Laura is spending the night here,' she said, by way of explanation.

'Who? Oh – Laura Grey? What's she doing here?'

'She is getting ready to open her shop – we've been busy – and she is pretty whacked.'

'Too bad,' he said, and sat down at the table. 'Janet, I have something to tell you, and it can't wait.'

She felt her heart give a leap, and sat down opposite him.

'I won't beat about the bush – I want a divorce.'

'George! What are you saying? Why have you come back now?'

'Because I wanted to tell you as soon as possible.'

'But a divorce! Why? What's wrong?'

'I'm sorry, Janet.' An apology was rare, but she could see he was het up, as well he might be.

She couldn't believe what he was saying. He looked so familiar sitting there, her husband, in his dark suit, impeccably dressed, looking just as he had when he left last Monday morning.

'I should have told you before, but for the past two years I have been seeing someone – in the States, she is American—'

'George!' She collapsed back in her chair, sat open mouthed.

'Well, there it is, I am telling the truth. She is pregnant and we want to get married – and there it is in a nutshell.'

He finally looked at her, seeing her face drained of all colour, her eyes wide in shock and disbelief.

'I can't believe this,' she whispered. He wasn't the easiest of men to live with, but she had never envisaged this situation. He had never appeared to be a man who was interested in other women – too wrapped up in his business, whose headquarters were in the USA.

'She is not young,' he went on, 'and it is her first child.'

As if I care, thought Janet bitterly.

'That's why I am rushing things,' he said reasonably, as if he was discussing a business appointment.

'What do you expect me to say?' she asked bitterly.

He reached over to take her hand, but she brushed him away.

'Oh, don't go all sentimental over me after all this time. You'll get your own way – you always do, and it looks as if I will be well rid of you.'

'I know I haven't been the best husband in the world – but I am being straight with you. There has never been anyone else, Janet.'

'And I am supposed to be pleased about that?' She stood up. 'What do you intend to do now?'

'Go to a hotel,' he said. 'I don't know what explanation you will give your – friend. And another thing, everything here will be yours, Janet. You have made this house a perfect home, and the divorce will be settled by a solicitor, but you won't lose out, I can assure you.'

'Oh, go away!' Janet said, in what was for her a very unusual mood. 'Just go – get out of my life!'

He hesitated for just a moment. 'I'll send for my things,' he said, and went out, closing the door softly behind him.

For a long time she sat staring into space, still not able to believe the conversation which had just transpired. Two hours ago, she had been having supper with Laura, thinking her husband was in New York and suddenly here she was, sitting at the kitchen table – her life changed utterly.

And then the tears suddenly came.

Laura lay awake for a long time, not hearing anything from downstairs – it was a large, well upholstered house – but hoping she would not be in the way now that George had come home. Finally, exhausted after her busy and exciting day, she slept.

She woke early, as she usually did, and lay thinking. There was no sound from anywhere, and she went into the bathroom next door, and with the lavishly furnished equipment, bathed, even washed her hair, before putting on her clothes, a little make-up, and going downstairs.

It was eight o'clock, and she found Janet in the kitchen.

'Good morning, Janet – I slept like a log, thank you,' she said.

But Janet had her back to her at the kitchen sink and when she turned Laura saw her face.

'Jan! What's wrong? What is it?'

She had obviously been weeping, looked drained as if she hadn't had a wink of sleep.

'Where's George?' she whispered. 'Has he gone already?'

'You could say that,' Janet said bitterly, and sat down heavily on a kitchen chair. She lifted her face. 'Yes, he's gone, Laura. Gone for good. How's that for an answer?'

They talked for a long time, going over and over the same thing, but at the end of it always the same conclusion. George had gone, and Janet was on her own.

Laura thought it could not have happened at a worse time, immersed as she was in the opening of the gallery. The party also, but Janet had said she certainly wouldn't be going to that. The victim of a broken marriage herself, but at least she had her son, Laura knew how difficult it was to take one's place in society and act normally.

She had to get back to Belford and clear things up in time for the removal men to move her own things out the following week to Cedar Green, and despite the trouble with Janet, found herself excited at the thought. She wished Jamie had been at home this weekend.

Driving to the gallery first, she checked that everything was in order before going home to finalize the move, for she would be, she hoped, busy in the shop. Upstairs the attics had been cleared, and she cleaned and dusted them. She had done everything possible, and knew that the men would be coming in sometime next week to wrap the china and fragile things.

She looked around the house. How many years had she lived here? It had been her first house when she was married – Jamie was born here in the first year of her marriage. He had known no other home. But now he had embarked on a life of his own – university life and all that it entailed.

Edie Fisher would be going in this afternoon to polish the furniture in the gallery – she would probably stay late checking everything – it was such an exciting thing to do. A shop of one's own – but thoughts of Janet and what had happened kept intruding on her thoughts of the gallery. She must find some time to call in on her. Poor Janet – and what a swine to tell her in that way. Dashing home to give her the news of his lover's pregnancy – but, Laura thought, it had been a strange marriage. They were hardly ever together – he was always abroad, usually in the States, while all Janet did, besides belonging to various societies, was to keep that beautiful home polished and shining for visitors. Not much of a life.

When Lady Somerville received the invitation to the garden party, she was shocked rather than surprised. A garden party! And at her solicitor's house in the village – the one with the lovely garden. Well, kind of them to ask her, but really. What sort of garden party was it to be? For a charity, for there was no doubt that Barbara Faulkner was behind it. No – thank you, but no.

It was while she was having her lunch that she reminded herself that Graziella, her granddaughter – such a difficult word to accept – would be arriving to stay on the 27th of June – would it be a nice idea to get an invitation for her too?

She must think it over. There were all sorts of implications and perhaps explanations – and she would not want to be bothered by those. Still, it would be quite an idea for Graziella to get to know the village and the people – after all . . . and so her thoughts and doubts went on.

It was the next day that she made up her mind. She always believed in sleeping on decisions.

Her answer was to Mrs Barbara Faulkner.

> *Dear Barbara,*
>   *Thank you for your kind invitation to the tea party on Saturday. My granddaughter, Graziella, will be staying with me at that time, and it occurred to me to wonder if it would be possible to include her in your invitation.*
>   *I am sure she would love to come. Please let me know.*
>   *Best wishes,*
>   *Celia Somerville*

And she put it under her blotter until the next day. No point in doing anything in a hurry.

Twelve

On the Saturday morning of the party Barbara was surprised to receive a call from Vanessa Hastings. No mistaking that overly cultured voice.

'Barbara, it's Vanessa Hastings – just a quick word, I know you are busy.'

'I hope you are still coming?' Barbara began.

'Yes, I am looking forward to it. It is simply that a friend of mine, Benjamin Green, returned from the States yesterday and has asked me to lunch – and I wondered if I could bring him with me to your party – he is a relative of Daniel Green, who is buying my property.'

It shot through Barbara's mind that her brother would not approve – but she couldn't help that.

'Of course,' she said warmly. 'We shall look forward to seeing him.'

'Thank you so much,' purred Vanessa. It might be quite interesting, she thought. Good to have several strings to one's bow. And John would be there, surely – John, for whom she had always had a soft spot – and one never knew.

Humming to herself, she began to get ready for lunch.

Janet Weatherall decided that after all, she would go to the party. What else would she do with herself? She telephoned Laura and told her and Laura sounded pleased. Good old Janet – she would take this latest thing in her stride and be better off without him, although she had no idea what her life had been with him.

Satisfied that everything would be ready for opening on Monday – she would take flowers in on Sunday and have a nice display in the window – she was ready for the party, getting herself dressed in a long skirt and embroidered top . . .

There was music going when she and Janet arrived, and the

garden looked simply superb. In place of snowdrops were petunias and geraniums, whilst the long border held hydrangeas of every colour together with herbaceous plants. The lawn was like velvet and Barbara and a young girl Laura imagined to be John Paynter's daughter, stood on the terrace leading to the house welcoming visitors, and Laura went over to Barbara and was introduced to Janie.

'What a splendid idea!' she said to Barbara, who looked like the cat that got the cream. More people arrived whom Laura did not know and gradually the tea party began to take shape. A long table had been spread with a cloth and various cakes and a tea urn, where Edie Fisher stood serving tea to arrivals, although there were plenty of helpers on hand.

There was no sign yet of John Paynter, and Laura felt vaguely disappointed. Perhaps he was not coming. It did not seem his sort of thing – still, it was early yet.

More people arrived, most of whom Laura did not know, but they introduced themselves, it was that sort of party.

Music could be heard in the background – and Laura wandered around the garden while Janet talked to Sadie Thompson, and Edie was so busy at the tea table that she had hardly time to talk to anyone. The local shopkeepers tended to gather in a group, while Janie and her friends – there were five of them now – were happy enough eating the goodies that had been provided.

It was towards four thirty when Vanessa arrived with her friend, Benjamin Green, a well-dressed, good-looking man, while Vanessa herself had dressed almost for a royal garden party in a floating long dress and large hat. She did not experience the warm welcome she had hoped for, seeing herself as a lady bountiful having sold her property for use as a retirement home. Sadie – Edie thought – looked the most interesting person there. Confident, smiling, well dressed – no one need be lonely when Sadie was around – and the party was in full swing when John Paynter appeared on the steps beside his sister with a warm smile, as though he was enjoying the whole affair. Thanks, John, Barbara said inwardly, while he went around smiling at the guests deciding he would talk to those people he did not know very well before talking to his friends.

'John!' Vanessa gushed, going towards him, and putting her

face up for his kiss while Green followed in her wake like a trained poodle.

'John – this is Mr Green – he is on the board of the Greensward Company who are buying Heron Court.'

As if he did not know, thought John, holding out his hand. He was pleasantly surprised at the firm handshake, and glanced across at the gates, which were both open to allow a wheelchair through. A car and chauffeur were parked outside, now moving away, as the wheelchair made its entrance watched by several pairs of curious eyes. In the wheelchair, protected by a sunshade, was Lady Somerville, but it was the woman pushing her who got all the attention. John thought she must be the most beautiful woman he had ever seen. They came towards him, while Barbara came down the two steps of the terrace, and welcomed them. She was so delighted that her Ladyship had come, but this young woman – she certainly would make an impact, for she looked like a Hollywood film star and almost out of place in a small English village.

'Barbara,' murmured Lady Somerville.

'Oh, how nice that you came!' Barbara said. She was delighted.

'And this is my granddaughter – Graziella. She is staying with me.'

To say Barbara was shocked was an understatement. This beautiful young woman. Her granddaughter!

'How do you do?' She put out her hand. 'Welcome to Cedar Green.'

Graziella smiled – and what a smile! Everyone there, whose eyes were on her, were warmed by that smile.

'Let me take you round and introduce you,' Barbara said now. 'May I?' and she took the wheelchair out of Graziella hands, thus leaving her free to mix.

Graziella took in the situation at a glance, a local affair – nothing in the least like an Italian gathering, but imagine – this was part of her father's background.

John came forward and took over. It was the least he could do.

'Hallo, I am John Paynter,' he said. 'Barbara is my sister and I understand you are Lady Somerville's granddaughter.'

Graziella smiled her wonderful smile. 'Yes, I live in Italy.'

Well, he would not probe, and they walked over to where Sadie Thompson was talking to her brother.

'Allow me to introduce—' John went on, turning to Graziella, thinking she might give her full name, but she smiled instead.

'Graziella,' she smiled. 'I am visiting my grandmother.'

From her position by the flower beds, Laura turned – oh, what a beauty! – and looked around for Janet, who seemed to have disappeared. She walked slowly towards the tree at the side of the garden, whose rich dark and shining leaves made a canopy of shade. She stood looking up at it for a long time, when John Paynter suddenly appeared at her side.

She smiled up at him. 'A strawberry tree, Mr Paynter,' she said. 'How nice to see – they are not very common, are they?'

'John,' he said, holding out his hand. 'Nice to see you. Nice that you know its name, too.'

'I love them,' she said. 'I had one, just a small one, in my garden at Belford, but this is a beauty.'

'My wife and I planted it when we first came to live here,' he said, and she threw him a look, seeing the expression on his face. How sad . . .

'So – er – how is it coming along – your new design for living?' John asked.

'Laura,' she said. 'Please. Well, do you know I am almost ready, and I can't wait now. It is so exciting.' She looked around, seeing Janie talking to her aunt. The girl's face was radiant.

'Your daughter looks very happy,' she said. 'I wish my son Jamie could have been here – but I am afraid not this weekend – but he will be with me next weekend, and I will be so pleased to see him. I can do with his help.'

You had to hand it to her, he thought, it needed some pluck to do what she was about to do.

He looked around. 'Ah, come and meet the Cattlins – have you met them before?'

'No, although I know he owns the antiques shop.'

'They are a charming couple,' John said, 'a real asset to the village.'

Dirk Cattlin was a shortish man, warm and friendly with an accent which she recognized as Dutch. Mamie was a pretty woman, an obvious American by her accent, who greeted her warmly.

'Oh, I do wish you luck in your new venture,' she said. 'Business is not that wonderful – but you know a little competition might do us both good,' and her laughing blue eyes put Laura at ease.

'You must come to us if you have any problems,' she said. 'Simply because we have been there a long time – and know the ropes,' and she smiled.

'Thank you,' and Laura found herself relaxing talking to this friendly woman.

'I don't think I am a going to be a threat to you,' she said. 'I have quite a bit of stuff from my parents' old home, which I need to sell – good stuff. After that – it will be the usual things. I like to think I have an eye for a bargain – and I am looking forward to it.'

'Well, we wish you luck,' Mamie said, and Dirk smiled at her and shook hands.

When they had gone a little way, Dirk spoke for the first time. 'I don't think she has a clue what she is in for,' he said.

'She's tough,' Mamie said. 'The thing is, honey, she is doing it for enjoyment – she is excited about it – I almost envy her.'

'Time will tell,' Dirk said, but he smiled.

Looking around for Janet, Laura still could not see her. Surely she wouldn't have gone home without saying something?

A tall, slim woman came towards her with outstretched hand.

'Hallo, I'm Greta Nelson. I have the only dress shop in the village.'

'Oh, hello,' Laura said.

'How are you feeling? As nervous as I was when I first opened?'

'Yes, well, it's all a bit of a dream really, I can't imagine I really open on Monday.'

'You'll be looking back on this in no time,' Greta said. 'It's quite interesting – this village life – more going on than you would think.'

'Well, I am used to it,' Laura said. 'I live – or did – in Belford.'

'Oh, so you know what it's like. It was a shock to me – I came from London – but well, I wouldn't go back now for the world.'

'That's nice to know.' Laura smiled.

'I'll pop along and see you when you've settled down,' Greta said.

'That would be nice,' and Laura watched her go and mingle with the other guests.

Suddenly she saw Janet emerge from the house – she had obviously been to the bathroom – and she had her sunglasses on, which possibly meant she had been crying a little.

Poor Janet, it was hard to see what sort of future lay in front of her.

She hurried over to her. 'Janet, love, everything OK?'

'OK,' she said. 'It was a good thing – today, I mean. I should have felt awful being home on my own.'

Laura took her arm. 'Yes, let's wander. So who have you met?'

'Well, I've been looking at the beauty – over there with the old lady.'

'Isn't she stunning? Apparently the old lady is Lady Somerville, and that is her granddaughter from Italy.'

'She looks Italian, like Sophia Loren.'

'Yes, you're right.'

Laura saw John approaching them, holding his daughter by the hand.

'Laura, I'd like you to meet my daughter, Janie.'

'How do you do?' Laura said. What a nice young girl – and with no mother – Barbara had told her. How sad. She was a fresh-faced, fair-haired girl, slim – but friendly.

'So you are reopening the Turners' old shop – are you excited?' Janie's eyes shone.

'Yes, I am,' Laura said. 'Monday, as it happens.'

'Oh, it's exciting for Cedar Green – it's always been such a dumpy end down there – oh, I'm sorry, I mean—'

Laura laughed. 'I do know what you mean, but let's hope I bring some life to it. I shall try, I can tell you. I am looking forward to it.'

'John!' Barbara called, and he excused himself and left them to talk.

They were soon joined by the attractive woman introduced as Dr Sadie Thompson.

'Well, my dear,' Sadie said. 'I am going to wish you the best of luck in your new venture.'

'Thank you.'

'Call me Sadie. You know I am going to be a new resident in this village, and I intend to take an active part in the village life,' and holding her arm, she walked Laura off, still talking. Edie, watching her progress, was so proud of her.

More people came up as they walked around the garden, admiring the flowers and the small flowering bushes and the little copse shaded by trees.

Presently, looking up, Sadie saw a large car arriving with her son Daniel driving. He parked in the car park alongside the house, and she hurried over to him.

'Daniel! I thought you were never coming!'

'So did I!' he said, and laughed. 'But well, here I am – how's it going?'

'Great,' she said. 'Ben is here.'

Glancing at her watch, Barbara saw that it was five thirty and she thought, Time for a toast.

She went across and had a word with John, and soon they disappeared. As Edie left the tea table, and mingled with the crowd, she couldn't remember when she had enjoyed anything more.

As Barbara walked towards the house, she saw the couple who ran the pharmacy, Bob and Margaret McAllister, who had waited until their shop closed. They were old friends. With them was Robert Doughty, a widower, a golfing friend of John's.

'I say, this is nice,' Margaret said in her strong Scots accent, 'what a splendid idea! Let's mingle, shall we?'

Around six Barbara disappeared with Edie and John and one or two ladies who had helped from the village, and emerged from the house with trays of glasses and champagne. The tea cups and urn and tea things were removed, and trays of glasses took their place. Bowls of nuts and nibbles of all kinds, olives and biscuits, were added.

John rapped quietly on the table with a fork, and soon everyone stopped talking.

'It is great to see you all here,' he said warmly. 'And thank you for coming.'

There was general applause.

'It occurs to me that we need some sort of excuse for a

gathering of this kind, and I suggest we raise our glasses to Laura Grey – who is going to open her new shop on Monday. Let us drink to its success. To Laura Grey.'

And he began to pour the first glasses of champagne for the women to hand around.

'Good luck, Laura!' came from all sides, and there was much talking and laughing and clapping of hands as Laura, flushed with excitement, walked over to the table.

Turning to the small gathering of local people, she thanked them.

'What a friendly village!' she said. 'I wish my son was here to share it with me, but thank you – John, and Barbara – all of you.'

Everyone now relaxed, eyes were turned towards Lady Somerville, who by now had left her wheelchair, and with the aid of a stick and her granddaughter's arm was slowly making her way towards Laura.

'Good luck, my dear,' she said, taking Laura's hand, while Graziella looked on. Tomorrow, she thought, I won't believe this really happened. Tea in an English village – and a newly discovered grandmother. Life could be very interesting.

Mr Green, who had no idea who Graziella was until Sadie told him, went over to her, leaving Vanessa to stare after him. She was well aware of the beauty by the elderly lady's side, and followed slowly after him. She knew Lady Somerville by sight, but had never met her socially. Now, she thought, was a chance to increase her social prestige. After all, think what she was doing for the future of the community.

'Lady Somerville,' she said. 'Vanessa Hastings – I live at Heron Court.'

Lady Somerville's hooded eyelids came down over sharp bright eyes. 'But not for long, I understand?' she said.

Slightly taken aback, Vanessa gave her a sad smile, as Graziella watched the little scene. She had summed up Vanessa in a flash. She had met many such women.

Benjamin Green had not taken his eyes off the Italian girl. It seemed to him that England was full of these beautiful young women.

'Sadly, no,' she said. 'I am going to miss it.'

'Are you leaving the area?' Lady Somerville asked.

Vanessa threw a swift glance at Ben. 'I am not quite sure yet – your Ladyship,' she said.

Lady Somerville gave a brief nod. 'Let us go,' she said, with a light pressure on Graziella's arm.

'Wretched woman,' Lady Somerville said. 'Now I would like to meet the little girl – John Paynter's daughter. He lost his wife, you know, a few years ago, it was very sad.'

'How terrible,' Graziella murmured. 'This young girl over there?' and she led her grandmother over to the small group by the door.

'That's the girl,' her grandmother answered.

Her eyes starry, and flushed with excitement, Barbara sat with her first glass of champagne in the kitchen.

'Well,' John said, 'I hand it to you, Barbara. It was a great success – and I am sure everyone will remember it with pleasure.'

'Oh, I hope so,' Barbara said, as Janie stood with one arm round her.

'Certainly worth all the hard work you put into it – eh, Janie?'

Janie left her aunt's side and went over and hugged him.

'Oh, Daddy – you were wonderful,' she said.

Barbara thought so too – her only regret being that her son, Greg, and his wife Stella had not been there.

But she must look on the bright side.

Thirteen

On Sunday morning, Graziella sat with her grandmother in the drawing room of The White House.

Really, it was beautiful here – what more could you wish for? she asked herself.

Mrs Baker knocked on the door and brought in coffee, which she set on the table by the fireplace.

'I'll see to it, Mrs Baker,' said Graziella sweetly.

'Thank you, dear,' Lady Somerville said.

As they sat drinking coffee and partaking of biscuits, Graziella thought of the special day she had had yesterday.

'What a wonderful tea party it was,' she said, her beautiful eyes shining as she remembered it all.

'Yes, it was. I quite enjoyed it.'

'You must tell me about some of the people I met. A nice man, John Paynter.'

'He is a solicitor with a practice in Oxford,' Lady Somerville said. 'His wife died several years ago, leaving him with that sweet little girl – Janie, I think they call her. And Barbara. Barbara Faulkner – who organized it – is his sister. She's a widow, but she keeps busy, helping out in the village, all sorts of charities – there is always someone like her in an English village.'

'And the striking-looking woman – Vanessa something or other?'

Again that shut down look.

'Wretched woman. Has the nicest house in Cedar Green – well, apart from The White House. Recently lost her husband, now she has had to sell up. The rumour is that he was heavily in debt, but if he was, poor man, it was entirely her fault. Now, can you believe, she has sold her house, Heron Court – to developers for a retirement home. I shall protest strongly when it comes up – they are bound to notify us.'

'And the man with her?'

'I am not sure – someone she has met, I daresay. She will have an eye to the main chance, I expect.'

'And that nice little woman – was it in her honour that the party was given?'

'Well, not really – I think Barbara just wanted an excuse. Still, she has bought the Turners' old shop – a wreck of a shop – and is opening next week as an antiques shop – well, I wish her luck. I can't see her doing any business down that end.'

'John – Mr Paynter – has a lovely garden, hasn't he?'

'Yes, lovely – not as nice as this, of course, but he and his wife were both gardeners.'

'I was wondering – it is so nice to be staying with you – what would you like me to call you?'

Lady Somerville turned inquisitive eyes to hers. 'Call me?'

'Well, I can't keep calling you Lady Somerville – but Grandmother somehow doesn't seem right. Do they have a pet name in this country?'

'Yes, but not one that I would like,' the old lady said. 'Call me Celia – that's my name.'

Graziella was inwardly delighted.

'Celia,' she murmured. 'What a beautiful name.'

Edie Fisher was trying to soothe her daughter Mandy, who had got back from looking at an apartment in Dudley Court, just outside Cedar Green. Mandy was in tears.

'So tell me what happened,' Edie said, putting the kettle on.

'Well, when I got to the agent's, he said he was very sorry but someone else had pipped me to the apartment. He was very sorry, but these things sometimes happen.'

'That's illegal, isn't it?' Edie asked, who knew nothing whatsoever about it.

'No.' Mandy was irritated. 'He'd seen it before me, anyway, but he came up with this offer and where I'd offered a bit less, he offered the asking price.'

Edie frowned. It sounded complicated.

'But you would have paid what they asked,' she said.

'I know, Mum, but he got there first, and the solicitors are already drawing up the contract. Oh!' she wailed. 'It was a super flat. I wish you could have seen it.'

'Good thing I didn't then,' Edie said, anxious to smooth over the difficulties. 'There'll be another one,' she consoled her.

'Not like that, there won't,' Mandy said, 'it was really special.'

'Who is he? Do you know?'

'What does it matter?' Mandy said. 'He's a widower – lost his wife a year ago, and he's moving out of a house into an apartment.'

'Well . . .' Edie began.

'I mean, what does he want a three-bedroomed, two bathroom apartment for?'

'Perhaps he has a visiting family,' Edie said, anxious to appease.

'Oh, if you'd seen it! The river view, the large rooms, the fireplace – the agent said it was the best one in Dudley Court. There'll never be another one like it, I know.'

'Now – you're just looking on the black side,' Edie said, making the tea. 'You see, sometimes these things are all for the best. They happen for a—'

Mandy blew her nose loudly, thus shutting out Edie's words.

'Here, have a nice cup of tea,' Edie said.

'Where's Tom?' Mandy asked.

'Gone to watch football with Tony,' Edie said.

'Well, I've got to find something soon, Mum,' Mandy grumbled. 'That would have been just perfect. Somewhere nice for Tom to bring his friends, you know, a really nice setting, like he is entitled to, you know, Mum. I mean, next year—'

'I know, love,' Edie said. 'Have a scone and butter – I made them for Tom's tea.'

'Lovely,' Mandy said.

It was ten minutes past ten when the shop bell rang, and turning from where she was dusting little figures on the shelf, Laura saw a woman she thought she recognized.

'Hi!' the woman said, smiling broadly.

Standing there, unless she was mistaken, was Pat Mackay, holding a bunch of chrysanths.

'Oh! Pat – Pat Mackay!'

'I thought I'd just pop in and wish you luck.'

'How nice of you – are these for me?'

'Well, of course, sweetie.' She looked around. 'My, but it does look good! Full of stuff – that's the ticket – knock 'em cold.'

She came forward and gave the flowers to Laura. 'I'll put them in a vase for you – Where's the sink?'

'Thanks – in the kitchen.'

'You don't want to leave the shop in case anyone comes in – what time did you open?'

'Ten – I thought I'd do from ten to four thirty every day. Mondays off in future and Saturday afternoon.'

Pat made a face. 'I don't know about the Saturday afternoon bit – that's when the tourists often come.'

'Well, we will see – I don't imagine I will be overburdened with customers all day – I have no illusions.'

'No, it's not that sort of shop – salon – if you don't mind my saying so, not to be confused with a newsagent's or a greengrocer's.' She looked around approvingly at the pictures on the walls.

Laura laughed.

'And you certainly will need Mondays – for buying. What time are you going to get for auctions and house sales?'

'I can't imagine,' Laura said ruefully. Now that she was open, she realized how much she had taken on.

If, for instance, people bought the large pieces of furniture how would she replace them? By going out buying of course – but would she have the time? John Paynter had been right – she hadn't really thought it through.

Anyway, up to now, her first customer was Pat Mackay – and she began to wonder how useful she might be. She had met her briefly at village affairs, and car boot sales – and Janet stuck to her guns that she was going to need someone like Pat.

No sooner had Pat disappeared into the kitchen than the little bell went again, and in came the Cattlins – both of them, Dirk and Mamie.

Smiling warmly, they both greeted her, Mamie holding a small pot of roses.

'We've come to wish you luck – and, of course, to look around.' And she winked. Dirk was already looking hard at the small Sheraton commode. He bent down and looked underneath, fingering the top. He was interested, of that there was no doubt. But Mamie kept Laura talking.

'Are you excited?' she asked. Then without waiting for a reply, 'You have some fine things in here.'

'Mostly from my family home,' Laura said. 'I've had them ever since my parents died – but they have to go sometime.'

By now Dirk had his eyeglass out, and was closely examining the back of the commode. There was no sound from the kitchen, and Laura guessed Pat was keeping quiet and out of the way.

Dirk looked around the shop and then went back to the commode. Now he was bending down to see underneath.

'Well, I must say, I think you've done wonders with the shop,' Mamie said. 'Who would have thought it was—'

'Mamie!' came from Dirk, who beckoned her over.

She joined him, looking down with approval at the piece of furniture.

'Nice,' she said, smoothing her hands over the polished surface.

He turned the price ticket over. 'What do you think?'

Mamie said nothing but nodded.

He looked across at Laura, whose heart had begun to beat quite fast.

'Trade?' he said.

'Of course,' she said, having found out what the usual trade figure was on items she might sell to another dealer.

'It's beautiful,' Mamie said, and you could tell that she really thought so.

He got out his pocket book.

'Cash,' he said. Laura was not surprised. She had learned a lot in the last three months travelling around locally.

He began to count out the notes – and Laura had a momentary, but only brief, flicker of sentiment as she remembered where it used to sit in her old family home. But not for long. She had made her first sale! And to them, of all people.

'We'll handle it,' Dirk said. 'I'll send the van down with Peter – Peter Knowles – do you know him?'

'No – I don't think I do . . .'

'He does all our collecting and deliveries – you might find him useful. Tomorrow all right?'

'Yes – morning or afternoon?'

'Morning,' Dirk said.

'Fine,' Laura said. 'Any time after ten – if that's convenient?'

'To suit you, honey,' Mamie said.

'Good luck!' she called over her shoulder as they left.

When they had finally gone, Pat emerged from the kitchen, her eyes shining with delight.

'Well! And you couldn't have had a finer first buyer!' she said. She went over to the commode and looked at the ticket.

'Well?' Laura said.

'A bit on the low side,' Pat said, and grinned. 'But then you'd guess that, dealing with the Cattlins.'

'Well, I'm pleased,' Laura said doggedly.

'You'll learn,' Pat said comfortably. 'Where would you like these?'

'On my desk,' Laura said firmly. 'They have brought me luck.' She glanced at her watch. 'Eleven thirty, and I have made my first sale!'

'Yes, well done – and to the Cattlins. Still, you might be sure they would want to be the first to spy out the land.'

She looked around the shop. 'Not many pictures,' she said.

'That's because these are family pictures, and I don't know a lot about paintings.'

Pat raised her sandy brows.

'Might be a good idea to learn – go to sales, that sort of thing. And you could do with some watercolours.'

She looked hard at Laura, as if assessing her. 'You know, if you need any help, I would be glad—'

'Yes,' Laura said, 'thank you.'

'I don't want to push myself in, but if I saw something – I do go around quite a bit, for other dealers, car boots and fairs – also you can pick up a bargain sometimes in charity shops, or small antiques shops in Oxford.'

'Yes, I often have,' Laura said. She didn't want Pat to think she was an utter novice. Looking at her now, in her jeans and jacket, her sandy coloured hair cut short, fair skin devoid of make-up, Laura decided she would be a fool not to take advantage of Pat's expertise.

'It's jolly nice of you to offer to help – I would be glad of it, especially when I run short and don't have the time to attend sales.'

'I'll always do a stint in here if you wanted me to – you only have to ask – oh, and by the way, I do know what I'm talking about: my father had an antiques shop in Tunbridge Wells, I was brought up there.' And she smiled.

'Oh, well, then,' said Laura, and she laughed, 'you can't say fairer than that.'

'Shall I make us come coffee?' Pat asked.

'Lovely idea,' said Laura, and found she really meant what she said. She was going to be grateful to this woman.

'So, Janet tells me you are actually moving in here at the weekend – from your house, I mean?'

'Yes – I shall go home every night this week – and be sure to lock up properly after me. My son will help me move – he'll be home that weekend.'

'Lucky you,' Pat said. 'To have a son, I mean.'

There seemed no reply to this.

From time to time several people stopped and looked in the window, at the furniture, the china and several interesting items, then walked on.

'Well, it's not a supermarket,' Pat said. 'It will take time to get established.'

'I can wait,' Laura said.

It was Monday afternoon, and Janie rushed home from school to call in on her auntie Barbara.

She found her in the garden, weeding.

She ran up to her and kissed her, hugging her tightly to and fro, she finally released her.

'Oh, wasn't that a splendid party on Saturday!' she cried. 'You must have been pleased – everyone enjoyed it so much, even Daddy.'

'Yes, he phoned me yesterday – I was quite surprised.'

'Well, there were so many people there – I didn't imagine it was going to be like that – shall I put the kettle on?'

'Yes, please dear – I'm coming in now.'

Bless her, she thought, she was more than ever pleased that she had made the effort now. She had had many telephone calls since Saturday saying how much everyone had enjoyed it. So, it had all been worth while – even John seemed to have enjoyed himself.

Once in the kitchen, when Janie had been to the bathroom and put her school satchel in the cloakroom, they sat at the kitchen table.

Janie put her elbows on the table and leaned forward, her blue eyes sparkling.

'Were you pleased, Auntie Barbara?'

'Pleased, child? Of course I was. It was great, I just wish Greg and Stella had been there, but—'

'And?'

'Yes – well, I think they are away,' she said, referring to her son and his wife.

'And?' Janie's eyes sparkled. 'What about that Graziella – you know, Lady Somerville's granddaughter? No one even knew she had a granddaughter – what is her name? Mrs – what? What is a married lady in Italian?'

But Barbara was busy with her own thoughts.

'Well, wasn't she lovely, though? Like a film star.'

'She certainly was – is,' Barbara said, handing her the biscuits.

'Do you think she has come to live with Lady Somerville?'

Barbara was shocked. 'Oh, I shouldn't think so! She has just come for a visit – I think she is staying in Oxford.'

'And that Mrs Hastings – oh, I can't stand her!'

'Now Janie, you shouldn't talk like that about someone you don't really know.'

'Don't you ever do that, Auntie Barbara – dislike people for no good reason?'

Barbara laughed. 'Well, yes – it is a human failing – but she just has an unfortunate way with her . . .'

'I tell you who I did like – that lady who is opening up the antiques shop. We walked around the garden, and talked – she is so nice – and easy to talk to.'

'Yes, she is,' Barbara said slowly. 'She is opening today – I wonder how she is getting on.'

'Well,' and Janie spoke softly, 'I don't think she will do much business.'

'And what would you know about it, Miss?' Barbara said, but she smiled.

'Well, you know – there is already one antiques shop – and it's a good one, isn't it? Perhaps she is lonely.'

'She has a son.'

'But he is at university. Perhaps her husband died – like Mummy did – and she is alone, like Daddy.'

No point in telling her that the couple were divorced.

'Now – to business,' Barbara said briskly. 'What are your plans this week? Tennis lesson on Tuesday—'

'That lady – Mrs Weatherall – I've seen her before – she looked so sad, didn't she?'

Barbara, who had no idea of the problems facing her friend, realized that she *had* looked rather worried.

'Well, she is the sort of person who is never bubbly, joyful like some people, she is what you might call a serious-minded person.'

'I like her, though, I felt I wanted to cheer her up.'

'Did you go and speak to her?'

'No, I didn't – you know, there were so many nice ladies at that party . . .' She sat thinking, elbows on the table, hands under her chin. 'Do you think it possible—?'

Barbara looked at her sharply. 'Now what are you getting at?'

Janie raised an innocent face. 'Me? Nothing! Why?'

'Then collect your things and get going – you'll miss Edie if you don't hurry.'

For that was always a treat for her. A chat with Edie.

Edie sat waiting. She was ready to go, but she wanted to see Janie.

All the tidying up had been done on Saturday by the helpers, and Jim Pettisham had put in half a day to clear the garden.

For it had been a great turnout – and she wanted to talk to Janie about it.

How pleased she was that Sadie had turned up. Good old Sadie – she hadn't changed a bit, and her coming to live in Cedar Green was a real treat for Edie. It would give her something to look forward to when Mandy moved out.

She didn't like to think about it. but it was natural given the circumstances. Mandy who was about to change her lifestyle, and Edie knew that meant that ultimately she would have her own home, which was a natural thing for her to do, especially with the boy, bless his heart.

Still, there was a lot of water to flow under the bridge before the retirement home got built – but then perhaps Sadie would stay anyway. She hoped so.

* * *

By the next weekend Laura had moved lock, stock and barrel from Belford to Cedar Green. The week had been interesting, just for the type of people that came in and what they were looking for. No more furniture had been sold, but many small objects. An ornate French Victorian vase, a pair of brass candlesticks, and some interest shown in one of the pictures. It was the portrait of a woman, an Edwardian beauty, unsigned by the artist and unknown. Her father had bought it in an antiques shop in Cheltenham. She had an idea that the woman might be back for it, she had seemed so interested.

A Chinese teapot, two large matching Copeland plates, and a visit from Janet and Pat – all in all it had been an interesting week.

And she mustn't forget the man, middle-aged, who came in with a small watercolour. It seems he painted watercolours, and wondered if there might be a market for them.

Pat Mackay was very interested. She thought the small watercolour was exquisite.

'What did you decide?' she asked, always curious as to what Laura would do.

'I suggested he asked what he wanted for it, and if I agreed, I would hang it and if it was sold he would pay me a commission. How's that?'

'Excellent,' Pat said. 'And I daresay there are plenty more where that came from.'

'I imagine,' Laura said, not telling either of them that she had thought the man rather nice, attractive, and she had no desire to reject his interesting painting. It would look very nice on the wall, and who knew, it might sell . . .

When Pat had gone, she and Janet got down to the business involving the break-up of Janet's marriage.

Janet looked awful. Pale and drawn, she wandered around the shop, picking up things, putting them down.

Suddenly she burst into tears, hurrying into the kitchen. Laura looked after her – had she really been fond of that ghastly man? For she had thought he was – whenever she had met him, she found him difficult, never showing any fondness for Janet – but who was to know about other people's lives? When Janet returned from the kitchen, she was more in command of herself.

'I'm sorry, Laura, I shouldn't burden you with this – but,

well, as my best friend I know you will forgive me. I feel better now.'

'Are you really going to divorce him?'

'What else can I do? His – *lover* – is pregnant. They need to marry and to make a family out of it. Oh, if I had had children, this would never have happened. Or would it?'

Laura had her own opinion on that, but she tried to comfort Janet as best she could.

'So what are you going to do? You have the rest of your life to live – don't let this finish you – you have a great future in front of you.'

'Doing what? I was never trained for anything – never had to work, except on charities, that sort of thing. I married George when I was twenty.'

'I didn't know you were that young.'

'We wanted to create a beautiful home together – and this, I hope, we did. What do I do now? Give it all up?'

'You could – and travel the world, learn something, train for something. You are still young – fifty is the new forty, you know.'

Janet made an effort at smiling.

'I don't have your kind of courage,' she said.

'Of course you do, when the time arrives – you just have to get on with it. Believe me – you will come to see this as a turning point in your life, and for the better – you'll see.'

She was talking out of the back of her head, she knew, for she had no idea what Janet's life had been like with that man. Just because she had disliked him, it didn't mean that Janet saw him the same way.

'Anyway – what about lunch on Sunday? Jamie is going back in the morning, I thought we might go to that new restaurant just outside Oxford – what's it called?'

Janet was brighter now. 'Yes, let's – I'll look forward to that.'

Laura didn't reveal that she needed Sunday to put her house in order – quite literally.

'Um, Janet, did George come back the next day – for his things?'

'You bet,' Janet said, 'every damn thing – he cleared the house, packed up his car, and said someone would be coming on Wednesday for the rest. Which they did.'

'Oh, Janet!' Laura said. 'So now you really are on your own.'

'Yes, I am free – if you want to put it like that. And he has left me everything, Laura. Every stick and stone in the house and the house itself – I haven't a clue what to do next – except—'

'Except what?'

'Make a visit to John Paynter. He can be my solicitor from now on.'

Sadie Thompson was having lunch with Edie at her small cottage on Stable Row. Edie had cooked lunch and afterwards they sat outside in the small garden beneath the apple tree.

'This is lovely,' Sadie said. 'Tell me some more about your family, your husband.'

They spent a pleasant afternoon in this fashion until the subject of Heron Court came up.

'How is everything going? The sale, I mean,' Edie asked.

'Oh, very well – it's in the council's hands. But Edie—'

'What?'

'One thing worries me – my brother's friendship with that woman.'

'Who? Vanessa Hastings?' Edie asked. She might have known this was coming.

'Well, you know her better than I do – what's she up to?'

'Up to? Selling her home because her husband died.'

'Well, she had to, didn't she. She was heavily in debt, or so I've been told.'

'Sadie, that's not our business, is it? Water under the bridge and all that. Your brother saw the house, it was up for sale, and he has – hopefully – bought it.'

'Not so,' Sadie said firmly. 'He has become absolutely dotty about that woman. If you ask me, he has marriage in mind.'

'Oh, surely not! It's far too early to speculate about that.'

'Not if you knew him I like I do. He has already had two wives.'

'Oh,' Edie said. There was no answer to that.

'What is she up to?'

Edie poured some more coffee. 'Now how would I know, Sadie? I'm not exactly in her circle.'

'I am very glad to hear it,' Sadie said grimly. 'I don't trust her an inch.' And she sat back, her lips compressed into a thin line.

'Well,' and Edie, true to form, was saying nothing. 'You don't know her, really, Sadie,' she said. 'You've only met her once.'

'And that was enough!' Sadie said grimly. 'You're a good judge of character, Edie – I should hate to see him get mixed up with someone like that.'

'Like what?' Edie sharply.

'Well, you know – conniving.'

'You don't know that,' Edie said. She suddenly felt like digging her heels in. After all, she had never liked Mrs Hastings, but that was no reason to.

'Anyway, that's enough of that,' Sadie said. 'When's your next half-day? I thought you could show me around Oxford.'

'Good idea,' Edie said. 'Let's fix it.'

Fourteen

Graziella was sitting in her bedroom overlooking the garden. She could see old Jim Pettisham busy along the flower beds. She had been pondering the best way to ensure that she could come here to live for good.

After all, why not? She had to be her grandmother's nearest and dearest relative – what was the point of going back to Italy? Italy was finished for her – an ex-husband, both parents dead, and a loving grandmother here in England with a beautiful house and presumably money – besides, she might marry again.

But how to go about achieving this?

She was due back home at the weekend – Celia knew this, but had made no effort to detain her. Perhaps she would remind her of it at tea time, after they had been for a drive. If she played her cards well she was sure she could engineer something . . .

It was a lovely day towards the end of July. Carter, the driver her grandmother hired to take her on drives, a retired man from the village, was on call. He drove her car, an old Bentley, which he looked after all the year round. It was his pride and joy.

Today they were going to the Cotswolds, not too far a journey for the old lady, and a stop for tea in Burford. It was a delightful run, through villages with little cottages resplendent with flowering gardens, pretty churches, and small shops – now and again an impressive large house would appear on the landscape where sheep grazed and the hedgerows were full of wild flowers. Oh, yes, she would love it here, Graziella thought – but she would need a man.

Still, she had never had any problem there.

When Carter parked the car, Lady Somerville put one hand

on her stick, Graziella proudly holding the other arm. It looked promising.

It was when they arrived home that Graziella decided to test the water, as it were.

'Celia, I cannot bear the thought of Friday and my return to Italy. I never imagined anything so beautiful as what we have seen today – although, I must say, Cedar Green, for me, will always hold wonderful memories.'

Although her sight was failing, Lady Somerville could swear there were tears in Graziella's eyes.

'My dear, do you *have* to go back so soon?'

Graziella sighed. 'Well, I still have a lot of clearing up to do – then, of course I must give up the apartment and find a smaller one.' She didn't add that her mother had owned it, and left it to her.

Lady Somerville's hand was on her arm in an instant.

'My dear! You must not even think of it! You are my grand-daughter – and I will not hear of it!'

Graziella's beautiful dark eyes filled with tears.

'Having found you – I am not going to let you go so easily! No, my dear – now, what would you think of coming to stay with me? Would it be too much of a culture shock?' And she smiled.

'Oh!' Graziella clasped her hands together. 'Do you really mean it? I could come to live with you?'

Her Ladyship looked almost as delighted as Graziella.

'Well, we should have to plan – work everything out. You could have the bedroom you are in and the room adjoining for a study or anyway a room of your own.'

Graziella was way ahead, picturing it.

'Would you have much – stuff – to bring over? Furniture, I mean?' she sounded doubtful.

'Oh, no! There is nothing in the apartment – furniture I mean, that I would bring here.' She had a momentary vision of the draperies and the silks and fringes and shawls and mirrors. 'Oh, no, just my personal things, quite a few clothes, and personal possessions.' I wouldn't leave those behind – where would I find anything so elegant over here? she thought.

Lady Somerville seemed pleased.

They sat in companionable silence for a while, Lady Somerville realizing she had an interesting future to look forward to – while Graziella was thinking it could not have been easier, the transition she had thought so difficult to achieve, now lay within her grasp.

At the end of July, Vanessa Hastings received a call from her daughter, Sarah. She was at Heathrow.

'Darling!' she gushed. She had almost forgotten the sound of her voice.

'I'll be home, soon,' Sarah said, 'just as long as it takes the taxi from Heathrow.'

Surely she could have caught a bus or a train, thought Vanessa, annoyed, knowing she would have to pay the bill.

She had been about to retire, but now she waited up, knowing that Sarah's room would be ready for her, no need for airing and heating in this hot weather.

For some reason she became quite agitated as the time passed. She had a lot of explaining to do. When Sarah had left it was soon after the funeral, and nothing had been done about the house.

When the taxi arrived, she saw it from the window coming up the drive with its lights on, so she went to the door to greet her daughter.

She saw a suntanned, fit young woman, bearing hardly any resemblance to the girl who had gone away a few months earlier. A young lady, very pretty, who flung her arms around her mother's neck and hugged her. This was not a very usual occurrence – they had never been close – but Vanessa held her close then stood her away to look at her, while the driver collected the luggage from the boot.

She settled the bill, and they went inside.

It could have been someone quite different from the girl who had left. She seemed no longer a girl of nineteen but a young woman, sure of herself.

Sarah went into the house, looking around as she did so.

'Oh! It seems so changed – half empty really. Have some of the things gone?' She seemed puzzled.

'Yes, I had to get rid of a lot of things,' Vanessa said sadly. 'It has been a very difficult time for me but come in – and what would you like? A drink – tea, coffee?'

'Tea, please, Mummy,' Sarah said, and eased off her jacket. Her arms were suntanned, and she looked the picture of health, totally different from the miserable girl who had left at the end of last year.

'You look wonderful, darling,' Vanessa said.

'I feel it – it was the best thing I have ever done.'

'Yes?' Vanessa turned on her way to the kitchen. 'Just let me put the kettle on.'

She returned in a minute or two. 'Now, tell me – how did you get on?'

'It was wonderful! And I might as well tell you straight off – I am going back!'

'Going back? What do you mean – to Africa?'

Sarah's eyes shone. 'Yes, Mummy!'

'But you can't – you're down for Bristol – you have a place!'

'Sorry – no way. I have found just what I wanted to do – not only for me, but helping other people as well. It is what I needed. Besides, I know Daddy would be pleased.'

A frown crossed Vanessa's face. 'Well, unfortunately, he is not here,' she said. 'What about your ambitions?'

'All gone now,' Sarah said, and she looked so happy and relaxed that Vanessa felt she was dealing with a new person.

'You wanted to do law,' she said.

'Well, now I don't – Mummy, there is a whole world out there. They need people, people like me who are willing to help. It is the most wonderful feeling when you know you are doing something to help the world's problems – no law degree can give you that. I have learned so much about myself.'

'Well, good,' Vanessa said, going off to make the tea and returning with a tray.

'But enough of me, for the moment – how have you been? I am so excited, I am forgetting what you have been through without Daddy. How have you managed? It must have been awful. I felt guilty at first for leaving you, then I became immersed in the work – and gradually put the sad memories behind me. But perhaps I shouldn't have left you – I was selfish—'

Vanessa, in her heart, wanted no change of plans.

'My dear girl,' she said, 'you have been simply wonderful, but as you can imagine – I have been so busy, with problems—'

'What sort of problems?'

Vanessa faced her. 'Money problems,' she said, 'and not easily solvable.'

'I don't understand,' Sarah said.

'Your father – Daddy – left this world heavily in debt, I am afraid.'

Sarah was shocked. 'What – what do you mean?' she whispered.

'What I say. We – or he – was in debt up to his ears, with the result that I have had to put Heron Court on the market.'

For the first time, she saw a touch of the old Sarah. Underneath the tan, she had paled and her eyes were wide.

'Poor Daddy,' she whispered.

'Poor Daddy!' Vanessa said. 'Can you imagine what it has been like for *me*?'

And suddenly, Sarah did. She knew what her mother was. Her demanding ways, and her lovely father, anxious to please – he had obviously overdone things.

'Oh, Mummy! I am sorry,' she said. 'How awful for you!'

Vanessa sat up straight.

'Heron Court has been sold,' and at this, Sarah gave a little cry.

'Mummy! Sold! How could – I mean – oh, how awful – where will you go?'

Vanessa sighed. 'Well, that's the problem. I had no alternative. The bailiffs came in – and well, I won't bore you with that tonight but that's what happened. Drink your tea, and we will talk about it in the morning.'

Presently Sarah looked up. 'Mummy, why didn't you let me know? I would have come home.'

'What could you do? The damage had been done by the time you left – you were better staying where you were.'

'And you have had all this to deal with on your own. I can imagine – you love this house.'

'Yes, I do – or did,' Vanessa said. 'It is no longer mine.'

'Who bought it? You mean it has really been sold?'

'Yes, a firm called Greensward – they are turning it into a retirement home.'

But Sarah's mouth was a round 'O'. She had not been prepared for a single word her mother had said. Only one thought stayed with her. Her beloved father – poor Daddy – what he must have gone through . . .

She stood up suddenly.

'I am absolutely whacked,' she said. 'I'd like to go to bed. Can we talk about this in the morning?'

On her way up the splendid staircase, she looked back at her mother. 'Is Edie still with us?'

'For the moment,' Vanessa said. 'But not for long.'

Edie was getting ready for bed when Mandy came in. She looked radiant.

Dressed in a well-cut black suit and wearing a white blouse, she looked every bit as smart, Edie thought, as those two Ledsham girls.

'How did you get on?' she asked.

'Well,' Mandy said, 'it's not as nice as the other apartment – well, I knew it wouldn't be. It's at the other end of the house – the darker end. Smaller rooms, but I suppose that wouldn't matter. The fireplaces aren't as nice. Anyway,' she went on, 'I've decided to take it – to buy it, I mean.' And she laughed at her mother.

'Cost you an arm and a leg, I bet,' Edie said.

'But I can afford it, Mum,' Mandy said. 'I must have somewhere nice for Tom when he comes home from Eton – and Robert would be pleased, I know.'

'Fancy it all turning out like this,' Edie said, putting the kettle on and getting out cups and saucers.

'Anyway, I'm worth it,' Mandy said, and they both laughed out loud.

'Seriously, Mum – I'm really pleased. Of course, I'll need some nice furniture – can't take what I've got.'

'Of course you can't,' Edie said. 'It'll be nice to look around the shops for antique things.'

They would both enjoy that.

Fifteen

By August, the little antiques shop was well under way. Laura had adapted her life to the running of the shop, and both Janet and Pat Mackay had done their bit. Once or twice, Laura went off to house sales or an auction while Pat looked after the shop, which she loved doing. She often brought in things for Laura's consideration, and even Janet found herself helping out more than once.

On the second day of her school holidays, Janie Paynter asked Edie if she could walk along the High Street to see Laura Grey's new shop.

She had to admit it looked very nice from outside, tubs of bay trees either side of the door, while inside it looked most inviting. Red walls, and it was full of objects of interest.

She entered the shop, and the little bell pinged, and Laura emerged from the kitchen.

'Oh, Janie! How nice to see you.' She smiled warmly.

'Mrs Grey,' Janie said, but Laura hushed her.

'Call me Laura – Grey was my maiden name. I am divorced from Mr Farrell.' She knew Janie would appreciate plain speaking, and thought, not for the first time, what a nice girl she was, intelligent, and how kind of her to come to see the shop.

'Look around, Janie,' she said. 'I have some nice things – but I am not expecting you to buy – most people don't, you know, they come in to browse.'

'Thank you,' Janie murmured, picking up small articles, and looking at the marks underneath. 'I know that's what you have to do – I've been with Auntie Barbara.'

'Oh, your nice auntie . . .'

Janie smiled. 'She has looked after me since Mummy died – well, her and Daddy – and of course Edie.'

'Oh, Edie.' And Laura smiled. 'What would we all do without Edie?'

Janie's eye fell on the small watercolour.

'Oh,' she said. 'Isn't that lovely – I wish I could paint like that. Watercolours are my favourite.'

'An artist brings them in – on sale or return, as we say. I hope I sell it for him, for he has others as well.'

'Golly – how much is it?'

'Forty pounds to you and I'll forego my commission.' But she laughed.

'Afraid not,' Janie said, 'but I do love it.' Her eye was on the small table.

'What's this little jug?'

'It's Worcester – originally part of a tea service – but unfortunately there is only the jug left, at least when I found it at an antiques fair.'

'It must be jolly interesting – dealing in stuff like this.'

'I find it so – you're either hooked on it, or bored to tears.'

'Or into minimalism,' Janie said seriously.

Laura regarded her. 'Yes,' she said. 'Which do you prefer?'

'Oh, old-fashioned every time – that's why I like going to Auntie Barbara's – she's got such lovely old things.'

Laura smiled. 'Well, you must call in here any time you like,' she said. 'I shall always be glad to see you.'

'When I am older, I could serve in the shop,' Janie said.

'I expect you will be at university by then,' Laura said, and smiled.

Janie stayed with Laura for half an hour, loath to go home, until the door opened, and a woman who looked vaguely familiar to Laura came in. Her eyes went immediately to the painting of the Edwardian lady.

'Good afternoon,' she said. 'Oh, I am so glad – it is still here.'

Ah, Laura thought. A sale.

'I would have been back before but I have been away on holiday,' she said. 'The painting is – fascinating. I was telling my husband about it.'

She eyed Laura keenly.

'Do you know its history?'

'I am afraid I don't,' Laura said. 'It has been in my family for oh, twenty-five years, I would think.'

'Do you know who she is?' the woman asked.

'No,' said Laura, and shook her head. 'I am sorry to be so unhelpful,' she added.

The woman went over and looked at it closely.

'Have you had much interest in it?'

They hadn't but Laura was not going to say so.

'Yes, quite a bit – she is rather lovely, isn't she?'

'Look,' and the woman seemed hesitant. 'I am very interested, but I would like my husband to see it, and he is away – he is in Chicago at the moment on business. I wonder, would it be possible to reserve it for me? I am sure he will agree to our buying it . . .'

'For a deposit, yes,' Laura said. 'I have had quite a lot of interest in it,' which she had not, but still, business was business. 'I would reserve it for two weeks and would have to ask for a fifty-pound deposit.'

'Well, I told my husband about it and he was very keen – but as he was off on business, he didn't have much time. I suggested buying it, but it is very expensive, and if he didn't like it . . .'

'Well, as I say, I would be prepared to reserve it for you for, say, two weeks – for a fifty-pound deposit.'

'Oh, you are very kind.' And after ferreting in her handbag the lady held out fifty pounds in notes, for which Laura gave her a receipt.

She put the money in her cash box – and hoped for a sale. She had put quite a high price on the picture, sensing that it might be valuable. Pat Mackay had a friend who was an art expert – perhaps he could enlighten her.

She hoped she had done the right thing – Pat would tell her.

Just before Laura closed, a man came in carrying a parcel, and she recognized him immediately. He was an ex-actor who had retired with his wife to a neighbouring village. His wife still worked, sometimes in television, but she had not seen him in anything for a long time, and she couldn't recall his name.

'Good afternoon,' she said, thinking how much he had changed from the old days. His face was fuller, and he carried quite a bit of weight.

'Good afternoon,' he replied. He still had an attractive voice, and was very well spoken.

'How can I help you?' Laura said. She had an idea he was not going to buy anything.

He withdrew from the parcel, wrapped in tissue, three pieces of silver, and Laura's heart sank. She knew less than nothing about silver and he obviously wanted to sell.

'I wondered if you might be interested in these, this silver tea service,' he said. 'It is Victorian, but we – I – have no use for it now. We seldom used it anyway, and it just clutters up the place.'

Laura's heart sank. To give an estimate was more than she could face.

'Oh, very nice,' she said. 'But I am sorry to tell you, that silver is not my particular thing – but my friend who helps me out sometimes is an expert.'

He looked so disappointed, that she hastened to reassure him.

'Would you be prepared to leave them with me? She will be in tomorrow – and I could ask her then. Have you a price in mind?'

'Er – no,' he said. 'Perhaps I could bring them back tomorrow.'

'By all means.'

He wrapped them again and put them back in the bag.

'They would probably fetch quite a price at auction,' she said.

'Er – yes,' he said. 'But I will be in tomorrow – morning or afternoon?'

'Morning,' Laura said.

'Good day,' he said, and left the shop.

It did not take long for Vanessa to get used to Sarah being home, and for Sarah to get very bored. There was little to do around the house; the swimming pool was covered, not being used, and one or other of the Green family was often there.

She had been home for a few days when Benjamin Green called on her mother, with the news that the final planning permission meeting was to be held later that week.

Introduced to Sarah, he quickly summed up the situation. The girl had been an obvious Daddy's girl, and had no time for her mother. Jealous of her mother's beauty, he wouldn't wonder, since the girl, while attractive, had none of her mother's charisma.

He did, however, ask her to join them both for dinner, which did nothing for Sarah's mood, for she couldn't wait to get back to Africa. He had nothing but admiration for the girl and the work she had chosen to do, but knew things would be easier for him if she were out of the way.

'Isn't everyone going to be annoyed at a retirement home being built in Cedar Green?' she asked her mother over dinner.

'I am afraid they will have to get used to it,' Vanessa said, with an intimate smile at Ben. 'After all, these places are so necessary these days, there is a big demand for them – with people living longer and—'

'Daddy wouldn't have liked it,' Sarah said stubbornly.

'But then your daddy is not here – unfortunately,' Vanessa said. 'That being the reason the situation is as it is.'

Ben saw the girl's blue eyes fill with tears.

'Tell me about your work in Africa,' he said. 'I think young people are wonderful the way they rally round to help – for it must be extremely hard going.'

Grateful to him, Sarah began to tell him as the waiter brought up the wine and water, and then the starters to the meal. He was really quite nice, she thought, which was more than she could say for her mother. Her mother didn't give a fig that her father had died – she was sure of that – and she didn't deserve this man, whom it was fairly obvious she had got her eye on and he on her. Not only that, she thought, but she doesn't really care about me. She hasn't even asked what I do.

She gave a great sigh. She couldn't wait to get back to Africa. It was hard work, but infinitely preferable to this.

At home finally in Rome, Graziella flopped into a chair and kicked off her shoes. Who would have thought it? She closed her eyes and went back in her mind to the time she had spent with her grandmother.

I still can't believe it, she thought. It is less than a few months ago that I met her for the first time, and here I am contemplating going to live with her!

There would be so much to do – the selling of the apartment for one thing, but she didn't imagine it would take that long. It was a charming apartment, and sold with the various pieces of Italian and French furniture should fetch quite a sum. There was nothing she wanted to take – except her own personal belongings, and they were quite considerable. But it would all take time. She imagined she might be finished with it all by – the end of September? If the flat was sold there was nothing else to keep her here, and she certainly did not want any post coming to her from Rome which might arouse her grandmother's suspicions – about the sale of the flat, for instance. For whatever else she was, she was an astute old lady. And Graziella must be sure to have severed all connections with her ex-husband's family – she did not want them to know where she was.

No – she must make a final break.

As to the future – well, whatever happened, happened. If she met and married – if her grandmother died – she could still come back if she had a mind, but she had a feeling she would not want to. England drew her, like a magnet, because, she thought, I am half English. Perhaps there is more of my father in me than I thought.

How she would tackle the situation at The White House was another matter. She had plans for that. The cleaner woman, Edie, she could cope with her – but that Mrs Baker was another matter . . .

Still – everything had been set in motion, more than she could have hoped for. After all, it wasn't every day that you inherited a rich grandmother.

She unpacked her luggage, and had a shower. There had been no messages from the janitor – and little post.

A glass of wine and something to eat.

When she finally got to bed, she pulled the blinds against the sunset, which showed her Rome in all its glory, one last look at the panorama in front of her, then she flopped into bed.

England – here I come.

The following morning Laura was in the shop with Pat Mackay when the actor called again about the silver.

'Oh, no,' Pat muttered under her breath.

'Good morning,' she said, when he closed the door behind him, while Laura disappeared into the kitchen.

'I wondered if you would be interested in buying these?' and he fiddled with the parcel.

'Let me see,' Pat said, as he withdrew the teapot, milk jug and sugar basin from its wrappings.

It was fine silver, she saw, with a Birmingham 1893 mark, and she got out her magnifying glass to examine it carefully.

'Silver isn't fetching the price that it used to,' she said kindly, and saw the disappointment in his eyes.

'Do you really wish to sell the set?'

She looked at each piece in turn and then suggested a sum which seemed to please him.

'If you are not happy, I should take them to the silversmith in Oxford.'

'No – no, that's quite all right,' he said. 'It's time we let them go.'

'Well – have a think about it,' she said kindly, almost dismissing him, but he stood doggedly.

'That is the highest sum you can go to?'

'I am afraid so,' Pat said gently.

'Very well,' he said. 'I'll take it.'

'You would like cash, I imagine?' Pat said.

'Oh yes – please,' he said, and when she gave it to him hurriedly went out of the door.

'Thank you, Mr—' but he had gone, hurrying down the street as if someone was after him.

When Laura came back from the kitchen, she looked accusingly at Pat.

'That wasn't enough, was it?'

'It certainly was,' Pat said. 'Laura you are in business, remember.'

'I know,' Laura said miserably.

'You know who he was, don't you?'

'I couldn't remember his name.'

'The actor Barry MacFarlane – used to be in English films.'

'Oh yes, I know.'

'And he wants the money for booze – drink,' Pat said. 'He goes everywhere selling up their home. I don't know if it's with her approval – Nancy. I think he recognized me – but no matter. Couldn't you just tell by looking at him, he's a drinker, and he will be back – you see—'

'You'd better be here then, if it's with silver,' Laura said. Oh, she wasn't sure she liked this side of the business.

Carefully, taking each piece in turn, Pat examined it – taking a fresh duster and idly polishing it. Good thing it hadn't been left to Laura – she would have given him twice that amount.

'And another thing,' she went on. 'You should have asked much more of a deposit for that picture – it's worth quite a bit.'

'She said her husband would be back in two weeks.'

'Hmm, well, if they don't buy it, she's lost her deposit.'

'I know that,' Laura said irritably. What did Pat think she was? Some kind of moron?

On Monday morning, John Paynter had two clients to see. One at ten thirty, the other at twelve o'clock.

It was ten o'clock and going into the cloakroom and washing his hands, he looked at himself in the mirror. Not bad for an almost fifty-year-old – at least he had his hair, which had been thick and lustrous and was now turning grey. He took after his family – they had all had good hair. Nails scrubbed – women liked to see well kept hands – and a final look at his face. A good shave – a good-looking man confronted him in the mirror, well built, standing tall – he looked like a man in charge – which he was, he thought with satisfaction.

Once back in his office, he waited for Sheila to announce his next client.

A tap on the door and she came in.

'Mrs Weatherall, sir.'

She closed the door behind the client.

He held out his hand.

'Good morning, Mrs Weatherall. Please sit down.'

He was shocked by her appearance, although he did not know her well. Nevertheless, she looked thinner and drawn, and there was no expression in her eyes, a deadpan look, he would have called it.

'How can I help you?'

He kept what he hoped was a welcoming face, relaxed to give the client confidence, and from the corner of his eye could see she was shaking slightly.

'Would you like coffee?' he asked.

'No – no, thank you – I just had some outside – in your office.'

He sat back, relaxed, and hoped she would do the same.

'We met recently, did we not, at the tea party held in my garden?' He gave her a warm smile.

She began to relax.

'Yes, it was wonderful – we all enjoyed it so much.'

'I think we have met before,' he said, to put her at ease.

'Yes, we have. At my father's funeral. The reading of the will. You were my father's solicitor.'

'Yes, yes, of course,' although he had forgotten that. It was years ago when he was first made a partner. Now, of course, he owned the practice.

He waited.

'I won't beat about the bush, Mr Paynter, I wish to divorce my husband, and wondered if you would help me . . .'

He felt a slight sense of shock – although by now he was used to that – no wonder she was het-up.

'My husband's solicitors – our solicitors – are in Bedford Row, but I wish to change mine – and if you are agreeable, I would like you to take over my affairs.'

'Of course,' he murmured.

'My husband – George Weatherall – came home recently to announce that he had a – *lady friend*, shall we say – in the States, that she was pregnant and he wished to marry her. Thus, the divorce. I would like it to be as soon as possible. I understand he has left me the house, the contents and a considerable amount of money – but that is the least of my troubles. We had no children.' And her lip curled in what could only be called a sneer.

'My dear Mrs Weatherall,' John said. 'You must relax – and put yourself in my hands. If you are quite sure that this is your own decision?'

'Oh, quite sure,' she said coldly.

'Then,' he said, smiling across at her, 'shall we begin?'

His desk was cleared by the time Sheila announced his next client, and the door was opened wide to let a wheelchair in, and then closed softly behind her.

John got up at once and came over, taking her hand.

'Celia.'

'Good morning, John.' She removed her gloves slowly, then looked up at him, a small smile on her face.

'John, I wish to change my will.'

Sixteen

Edie had come into the shop on Saturday afternoon to dust and clean and on Sunday Laura took the opportunity of getting into the garden. This was something she had looked forward to for a long time and now she took stock.

A small rectangular lawn, surrounded by curved grass edges – she approved of that, but it was now hopelessly overgrown – and the borders were filled with shrubs and now, at this time of the year, it was a blaze of colour. A wisteria on one wall was now in full leaf, the flowers being almost over, while roses grew on the other walls. The climbing Lady Hillingdon she recognized, she had last seen that climbing over a wall at Wisley, and this one was hopelessly entangled, but she would look forward to coping with that. There were roses and old roses – she recognized some – in the overgrown beds; tall delphiniums in every shade of blue; hydrangeas; lupins; white phlox, one of her favourites, would be out soon, interspersed with lavender bushes and rosemary, and small elegant conifers – and on the opposite wall, which overlooked the lane, Virginia creeper had taken over, to drop prettily over the other side, while at the bottom of the garden stood a small fruit tree, possibly plum – and what she was more pleased to see than anything, a hawthorn tree, which in the spring would be ablaze with blossom, pink, red or white like tiny roses, which was barely fifteen feet tall, and had obviously been planted not too long ago. It was truly a cottage garden.

Standing back and surveying it all, she was more pleased than she thought possible. She had certainly not envisaged a shop *and* a garden.

For that was what she had always been – a gardener – the one thing she would miss from the other house – but would she now? This garden was big enough – and she surely would get help if she couldn't manage it, for she was determined that she was going to restore this small piece of land. It was hers – all hers. The last owners must have been sad to leave it.

With her gardening gloves on, she went to the small shed, where she had housed her gardening tools, shears and rake, Dutch hoe and spade, a quickening of her heartbeat telling her she had a day to herself – all to herself. She would enjoy every moment.

The borders needed to be cleared of weeds first, for the lawn could wait – and she set out with great fervour, the wheelbarrow at her side, one load followed another until she had two barrows full, and half the first border done.

She went indoors to make herself coffee, and sat outside in the sun on this glorious day, her sun hat rammed on her head, her gardening boots pulled over her jeans – not a speck of make-up – and felt on top of the world.

She started cutting back the climbing rose, Albertine, which would only flower once but was so pretty, and took the cuttings to the top of the garden, where she kept them separately from the compost heap. There was some fine compost there already, and she determined to use that and make a fresh one.

Pushing back the wheelbarrow she started clearing the soil, digging out the weeds, pulling them, until another barrow was full, which she tipped up to join the other. Cutting back extra growths on the wall, she discovered that the border was wider than she imagined – all of four feet – plenty to do when this border went round the garden and back to the kitchen door.

Soon after twelve, she made her way into the house, discarding her boots and going into the small cloakroom for a clean-up. She would continue after lunch and hope to get the whole border finished then a shower at the end of the day.

Going into the garden, and seating herself at the little wooden table with a small glass of white wine and her sandwiches, she wondered what Janet was doing with herself. She had insisted that she had plenty to do at home – I must get used to this single life, she had said. Laura thought it had not been that different when she was married – George was so often away.

She contemplated the border she had done – how nice it

was. Gardening was so rewarding, and for her it was a means
of relaxation.

It was after lunch that Janie made her suggestion.

'Daddy, couldn't we take a walk? It's a nice day . . .'

He looked at her. 'I thought you had a lot of prep to do?'

'I've done it,' she said. 'Oh, come on, Daddy – why don't
we go along the High Street and have a look at Laura's new
shop?'

He looked at her.

'She asked me to call her that. She said she is not Mrs
Farrell any more – and Grey was her name before she was
married.'

'Yes, yes, yes,' he said. 'But I thought you'd been to see it
before?'

'Yes, I have – and that's why I think you should see it too.
She has made a really good job of it.'

Why would he refuse? he wondered. He had been curious,
if he was honest. He normally never went down that end of
the High Street – and had never seen the shop since she had
done it up and taken over.

'Very well,' he said, pushing his chair back. 'Not a bad idea
– we could do with a nice walk,' and he went off, muttering
to himself, while Janie smiled. Goody!

It was a lovely afternoon. Wherever there were tubs they
were filled to overflowing with flowers – begonias, fuchsias,
geraniums – the whole of the High Street looked festive.

They walked slowly, joining the tourists and visitors, taking
it all in, John noticing the few changes that had been made,
and that somehow this end of the High Street had taken shape.
It looked different – as if it had had a new lease of life. Bay
trees in tubs stood outside the door of the shop and although
it was closed, it had quite a festive air, and one or two people
were looking in the window.

He looked across curiously, and waited for a car to pass
before they crossed the road, and joined the other two viewers.

'I like that little chair in the corner,' the woman said. 'Anthea
would like that – she is looking for a small chair.'

'I should phone and ask the price – or call in,' her companion
said. 'It's nice though, isn't it? Quite cheered up this end of
the village,' and they moved away.

John stared in at the window. It certainly was a nice little shop. Pretty, colourful, and full of objets d'art – one or two nice paintings on the dark red walls, pretty lamps, and an assortment of colourful china and glass – he had to admit he was surprised – could not imagine it when she had first told him of her plan.

'Oh look, there's an old teddy bear – look – sitting in that tiny chair, in the corner, Daddy.'

He looked at her. 'Would you like it?' he asked.

'No, not really – I have Busby.'

Bless her, he thought. Who knows what a young girl of her age is thinking half the time.

He decided to join in the adventure.

'Let's go round the corner – into Tinker's Lane,' he said.

She was delighted. Along the wall, the Virginia creeper fell over the gate, almost hiding it – and sounds came to them of someone in the garden, working.

Janie made a face.

'Laura must have found someone to do the garden,' she said. 'You can hear them working.'

But a memory of snowdrops in a large tub came back to John, snowdrops and a strawberry tree. He thought he knew who might be working in the garden.

He suddenly looked like a small boy, mischievous, knowing that nothing pleased Janie more than when he came down to her size.

'Shall we knock on the gate?' he said.

'Daddy!' Her eyes were glowing now with the idea they were conspirators working together.

'Yes, let's,' she said, eyes sparkling.

He rapped on the gate with his walking stick, and presently they realized that there was a silence. Whoever was working, had stopped.

'Perhaps it's old Mr Pettisham,' Janie said.

'No – I don't think so,' her father said.

'Who is it?' came a woman's voice.

'Laura,' whispered Janie.

'Hallo, Laura. It is John Paynter – and Janie. We've come to see how you are getting on.'

Which sounded to his ears slightly ridiculous, but in for a penny . . .

They heard the key turn in the lock and bolts being slid along, then the door was opened, and Laura stood looking at them in all her glory. Garden hat, old jeans, boots – dirty gloves.

'My dear – do forgive us – but we are being nosey,' he said, as she beckoned them inside.

'We just wanted to see the garden – and I, of course, I would like to have a peep at the shop – is that possible?'

Oh, how could he! Laura thought. Me – looking like this! How did I know that someone might call – and no ordinary visitor! But she managed a welcoming smile.

'Do come in.'

She recalled her mother's words. Never excuse yourself to unexpected visitors – after all, they are the intruders – not you.'

'This way,' she said, and smiled. Closing and locking the gate behind them, she led them into the garden.

John looked around, surprised. He had imagined a dump of a place, but apart from the lawn, the beds had been cleared, the rubbish neatly stowed away in the corner.

'I'll show you the garden first, and clean myself up when we go inside. It's time for tea – would you stay?'

Glancing down at Janie, and her excited face, he smiled back at Laura. 'Love to,' he said. 'This is very kind of you – Janie will give you a hand.'

'Not at all,' Laura said politely.

They walked round the garden looking at everything.

'John, you will find three folding chairs in the little shed – would you?'

'Of course.'

'Now, I will just be a few minutes to clean myself up – it is time I finished, anyway, I've been out here all day.'

'You take your time,' he said. 'We can wait. We are just out for a Sunday afternoon jaunt.'

When Laura emerged – cleaned up but still wearing her jeans, no garden hat, but shoes and a clean tee shirt – and a touch of lipstick, he noted – she was carrying a tray of tea and biscuits.

John felt remorseful.

'You know this is an awful cheek,' he said. 'It just seemed a good idea at the time . . .'

And Laura laughed. 'I think it's great. My first visitors – and my first day in the garden – it's a celebration tea, a garden open on Sunday.'

'You must go on the open day list,' John said.

Their eyes met for the briefest moment before she returned to the tray.

'Milk?' she asked.

'Yes, please,' they both said.

'There is no shade – and I haven't a sun umbrella. Is it too hot for you, Janie?'

'No,' Janie said, 'I'm fine.'

She took the tea things away into the kitchen, then turned back to Laura and her father.

'Laura, do you suppose Daddy could have a look at the shop?'

For some reason Laura flushed a fiery red.

'Of course,' she said, 'delighted to show you,' and led the way through the back door and past the little kitchen.

'Isn't this super, Daddy?'

He saw the small white kitchen, modernized with all facilities, blue check curtains at the window, flowers on the sill – Typical Laura, he thought.

On his left was a small door. 'And where does this lead?' he asked.

She opened it for him, and he saw a small cloakroom, and a modern shower.

'What an excellent idea!' he said. 'So useful.'

'Jamie thinks so, when he is home.'

'When is he due home next?'

'Next weekend,' and she smiled.

Closing the door, she then unlocked two separate locks, and switched off the alarm.

Once inside, he was astonished that the miserable little shop it had been could have been so transformed.

'My dear Laura!' he said. 'No wonder everyone is making such a fuss about it!' He could see she was as pleased as punch.

He looked around at the nice pieces of furniture, the two large windows, the pot plants – it was worthy of Bond Street, he thought, and felt tremendous pride for what she had done, though he couldn't imagine why.

Seventeen

It was August. Dry heat hung over everything, and the shop had been quite busy, but this was because the tourists came in droves.

The auction houses were quiet, as were the house sales, but Pat Mackay kept Laura busy with oddments she found from time to time and a Canadian couple who lived in Oxford bought the beautiful sideboard. Laura was a little sorry to see it go – it had been part of her childhood – but she reminded herself that this is what she was there for – and was pleased with the sale. This left a gap in the showroom which she filled with a William and Mary desk. She had saved this for Jamie but he had no interest in it, so she placed it in the shop, newly polished with a French clock on top of it. It had plenty of compartments for modern use, together with a secret drawer, and attracted quite a lot of attention.

The watercolour man sold his painting, and brought in two more – he was so delighted to find an outlet, and Laura began to wonder about the woman who was interested in the Edwardian painting. Had she changed her mind?

Having taken a day off that week to spend with Jamie before he went on a European holiday with his friends, she was pleased that Janet, with a little help from Pat, took over. It was the next day, a Wednesday, when the woman came in, accompanied by a dour-looking man who went straight over to the painting.

'Good afternoon,' the woman said. 'I called in before and left a deposit on the painting over there,' she said, pointing to the portrait, and the man nodded and extracted his wallet.

Her husband – or male friend – was staring hard at it. He brought out a magnifying glass and studied it carefully.

'May I?' he asked for permission to take it down.

'Of course,' Laura said.

He could not have been more thorough, and the woman watched him. Turning it over, he nodded to her, a gleam of satisfaction in his eyes.

'I thought he would,' she said, smiling at Laura.

'You have no idea who the sitter is?' he asked, which led Laura to think perhaps he knew something about art – probably more than she did.

'No, I'm sorry.'

'Do you know anything about its provenance?' he asked.

'No, I'm sorry – it has been in my family for – well, must be twenty-five years. My father bought it in an antiques shop.'

'Do you know where the antiques shop was?'

Why the question? she wondered.

'Yes, I think it was in Cheltenham.'

He nodded to the woman, who got out her purse and extracted a card. He shook his head.

'Cash?' he said to Laura.

'If you prefer,' she said. 'That's three hundred and seventy five pounds, less your deposit – shall we call it a round three hundred?'

'And I would like a receipt,' the man said.

She wrote out a receipt for the money, for the sale of an Edwardian painting by an unknown artist.

'Could I have your name?'

'Smith,' he said. 'Robert Smith.'

Having finished that, Laura went to the cupboard where she kept bills, oddments and wrapping paper, and wrapped it carefully, first in bubble wrap and then in brown paper.

It was the biggest sum of money she had ever taken.

Nowadays there was really never a day when a van or extra cars weren't in the drive at Heron Court.

Architects, surveyors, builders – they were everywhere, for they had been granted planning permission and life for Vanessa had really changed.

Greensward employees were everywhere, and Daniel Green had said Vanessa could stay put until they were really under way, which meant she must decide where to live, and what to do with the rest of her life.

Benjamin Green was due to call today – he had been in

London for the past few days on business. But Vanessa was distracted.

Move from Cedar Green – to where? London seemed the obvious choice, but she would have to make new friends – she had not lived in London since she was a girl, and then had married Stuart and come to live in Cedar Green.

Then again, she hoped to find a man – a single life was not for her, one man friend after another – she needed a man to take care of her, as she so sweetly told herself.

If she was honest, John Paynter was this man. She had had a soft spot for him ever since she had met him – he and Stuart had been such close friends. But a future with John – much as she was attracted to him – looked to her a bit bleak. Firstly, he had a teenage daughter to bring up – she could do without that, having just got rid of one. Then again, a solicitor?

What kind of money did that bring in? Very little, according to Vanessa's standards. He had a decent house, but it wasn't her sort of house – the very name, Churchgate House – it did not sound like her. But he was a – sexy – man, for want of a better word. There was just something about him. Tall, good-looking – a *strong* man. Stuart hadn't been strong – she could wind him round her little finger – but he had given her everything she wanted. On the other hand, life had been dull, the only excitement being acquiring something new. She wouldn't mind pitting her wits against John Paynter. It could make life quite exciting.

That evening, Ben came back from London, and took her out to dinner. He was obviously delighted to see her and waited for her in the drawing room. When she finally appeared she looked stunning, and he rose to greet her.

'You look wonderful,' he said, bending forward and kissing her. 'I have booked at The Fisherman,' he said, referring to a restaurant on the river noted for its good food.

She was delighted.

The evening was warm, and people were sitting about on the terrace overlooking the river, while swans and ducks sailed past – it was a beautiful scene.

They sat over their drinks while she asked him how he had got on in London. Studying him, she thought he was quite a man. Of good build, quite an impressive man, as he should be with his business record, and she wondered vaguely what being married to him would be like. That there would be money, was no question, but she knew little about him, what made him tick, except a strong business urge – she was not drawn to him physically as she was to John Paynter. He was also, she suspected, some ten years older than she was, but having had one shock in her life, being brought down to size, was enough for one lifetime.

Inside, over dinner, he told her of his day in London, and that the plans had progressed so well, that they were almost ready to start work at the end of the month.

'And now comes the question, my dear,' he said. 'What are you going to do?'

She had expected this – and was still not sure of her answer.

'I have told you, you may stay at Heron Court as long as it is possible, without them working all around you. The first part will be the building of the apartments – get that off the ground, redesign the gardens, before we actually tackle the interior of the house, which will be the most important part of the whole development.'

How she would hate that – builders, all over her wonderful home, knocking walls down – no, it was just not on.

'This will all take time – but have you made any plans? You could always have an apartment—' but saw her look of horror.

He hurried on: 'We shall be building small cottages, perhaps a dozen – but I don't imagine—?'

'No, Ben,' she said. 'I don't like the idea of staying anywhere near Heron Court – it has been my home for a long time, I can't bear to see it changed,' and she looked so sorrowful, he reached over and took her hand.

'But financially – forgive me, my dear – you will be able to afford to buy yourself something of your choice – but I do hope it won't be far away.'

The $64,000 question, she thought.

'Yes, I will have to make up my mind – I do not want to hang around while they destroy Heron Court – it has been my home, my dream home—' and her voice caught on the words, so that he took her hand again, but she withdrew it.

'I shall need a little more time, Ben,' she said, sweetly but wistfully. 'It is a big step for me to take – surely, you can understand? After losing . . .'

'Of course I can! I am not a hard man – but, well, we have to get on with the job. I have to be practical – and I want to see you settled.'

She lowered her lashes. How serious was he about her? Did he intend to ask her to marry him, for she would accept nothing less? And she was not sure about that, either.

She must collect herself and make plans and stick to them. After all, now she had some money – it had not all gone to the bailiffs – but there was not enough to keep her in the manner to which she was accustomed.

She leaned over and patted his arm.

'Dear Ben,' she said, 'you are a kind man, and I am very grateful for your concern.'

He looked her straight in the eyes.

'Why would I not be?' he asked gently. 'I am very fond of you Vanessa – in fact, perhaps I am speaking too soon—'

She lowered her eyes.

'Do you feel anything for me, Vanessa? Apart from friendship?'

She reached out and laid a hand over his.

'You have been very kind to me and I am so grateful – but it is early days, Ben. It was only last year . . .'

'I understand,' he said. 'I just want you to be settled – it has been so hard for you, being turfed out of your home – you don't deserve that.'

Too true, she thought – but if she could keep him dangling a little longer, until she made up her mind – after all, she did not want to lose him – there might be a time in the future . . .

'I think it is time we went,' she said.

'Yes,' he said, calling the waiter over for the bill, and collecting her silk scarf from the chair, putting it around her shoulders.

Having paid the bill he escorted her to the car.

'I shall be around from now on,' he said, 'so anything you need, just ask.'

'Thank you, Ben,' Vanessa said, settling herself in the large comfy passenger seat of the Mercedes.

Be sure I will, she thought.

'Edie,' Sadie said as they sat having coffee in Edie's little cottage. 'Are you still working at Heron Court?'

'Yes, until they tell me otherwise – but I don't suppose it will be long now. There will be heaps of work once they have finished, I probably wouldn't be able to cope with the demand – but at the moment, until Mrs Hastings moves out . . .'

'And when will that be?' Sadie asked.

'I've no idea – she doesn't confide in me,' Edie said cheerfully. 'Mrs Hamlett is leaving at the end of the month.'

'Is she the housekeeper?'

'Yes.'

Sadie put her cup down. 'Well, you know what's worrying me.'

'Oh, you're not still on about your brother and Mrs Hastings?'

'Well, wouldn't you be if he was your brother?'

'I think they're good friends – get on well together, you know.'

'Well, I think it's more than that. I know the way he talks about her, and if he is that keen he wouldn't think twice about asking her to marry him.'

And it would be the way out of her difficulties, thought Edie, but she said nothing.

'She will have to move out soon, I expect,' she said.

'Of course she will – and a good thing too.'

There was no getting round Sadie – she had her mind made up.

'I have put my name down for a flat in Heron Court,' Sadie said presently.

'Have you? Oh, that's great!' Edie said. She was so pleased. A childhood friend come to live in the same village – what more could you want?

Graziella stood looking around at the almost empty flat in Rome. Sold – with contents, such as she was prepared to leave.

Furniture and drapes, fitments and carpets – she had got a good price and she knew it. Had held out for it. A Greek gentleman – but these days whoever expected to sell to a fellow countryman? The world was changing. Soon every country in the world would be multi-national.

But it wasn't her problem – she was leaving, and she was excited, too. The apartment had sold more quickly than she had thought it would, but then good properties in good locations were in great demand. And look where she was going. A fair exchange? She thought so.

Her luggage was stacked in a small room, and she was due to fly out in two days' time.

This afternoon she would take a last look around the Via Veneto – although she would come back to visit, she well knew. She would have tea in the best hotel in Rome – and make the most of it.

She browsed around the wonderful shops – the great designers – but she needed nothing. Everything had been taken care of in that direction, even her grandmother's gift – a silk scarf from Valentino, and a small black Gucci handbag that was already packed, and she entered the luxurious hotel and made for the terrace.

Seating herself, she looked around – yes, it was beautiful – and she would miss it – but the time had come for another life, a new life.

She ordered China tea and biscuits, and was horrified when a soft Italian voice beside her said, 'Graziella – what are you doing here?'

She looked up to find her once-upon-a-time sister-in-law, Julietta – her ex-husband's sister – glaring resentfully down at her.

'Julietta,' she said, and indicated that she might sit down. Julietta gave her a scornful stare.

'What are you doing here? Were you not advised to keep out of Rome?'

'I am visiting – a brief visit. I am leaving tomorrow,' Graziella said.

'Be sure you do – or you will be sorry,' Julietta said, and head high, stalked out of the restaurant.

'Bitch,' Graziella said under her breath, knowing full well that one of the terms of the divorce was that she would leave Rome. She took her time, slowly finishing her tea and biscuits, then paying her bill, before she sauntered idly out of her favourite hotel, and back to the apartment.

She couldn't leave soon enough.

Edie had just left Janet's house, and Janet and Pat Mackay sat in the kitchen having tea.

Pat Mackay was very fond of Janet, but often became impatient with her, no more so than now, when she had almost gone to pieces after George left.

'You've got to do something with your life now George has gone,' she said. 'He is not, and never was, worth bothering about.'

She never minced her words.

'He was my husband, nevertheless,' Janet said, digging her heels in.

'Well, I'm sorry but you are better off without him – always away. And now you have learned he has another woman – and pregnant at that!'

'Oh, don't go on!' Janet said. 'I hate living alone, just hate it. It's all right for you.'

'Well, he wasn't often here, was he?'

'No, but my mother, who was widowed early in life, said you could put up with loneliness if you knew someone was coming in eventually – and that's the kind of life I lived with George.'

Pat sighed. 'Well, I live alone and I love it. I can please myself what I do, when I do.'

'Yes, but you're not me,' Janet said doggedly. 'Sorry – I know I am a bore.'

'I'd just like to see you pick up the pieces and live a decent life,' Pat said. 'After all, it has nothing to do with me, but as a friend . . .'

Janet looked around. 'I mean, this house has been my life for what – twenty years? We built it together, both of us, it was all we cared about, improving it, buying furniture for it – to us it was like a child, something to care for.'

'It replaced a child,' Pat said.

'If you like. I mean, Pat, what am I going to do with it all?'

'Well.' Pat took a deep breath. 'Do you want to keep all of it? Do you still want to live in it on your own?'

'I did live in it on my own, for years,' Janet said.

'Well, then carry on doing that – if that's what you want.' She picked up her handbag as if to go.

'Don't go,' Janet said. 'Tell me what to do.'

'How can I? We are of different temperaments – I would take a wonderful holiday, then sell up, get rid of it, and use the money to travel – or do something.'

'I'm not really interested in travel – I could have gone with George often, but I seldom did.'

'More's the pity,' said Pat. 'Things might have been different if you had . . . or try giving a hand to people less fortunate than yourself.'

'I do – I give money to charities.'

'That's not enough,' Pat said. 'You need help, too. Oh, come on, Janet – snap out of it, don't let him beat you.

'Anyway,' she went on, 'Laura will take all the stuff you want to get rid of – keep her going for years.' And suddenly they both saw the funny side of it, and laughed until they almost cried

Janet dried her eyes, half laughing, half crying. Then took a deep breath.

'Why don't I go in with Laura? Go into partnership with her? After all, she can't manage on her own, now, can she?'

Eighteen

Sophie Ledsham and Edie's daughter Mandy met up in Oxford – in the supermarket. They were at the fruit counter, and glanced at each other as they both chose apples, one paled and the other's cheeks went a fiery red.

Mandy stood in shock, open mouthed. It was the first time she had met a member of the Ledsham family since the funeral and the reading of the will, and for Sophie the first time she had met Mandy as the mother of her half-brother.

Sophie spoke first.

'Mandy . . .' she spoke softly and Mandy bit her lip. She had never felt so embarrassed in her life, but she was grateful that it was Sophie and not either of the other two. Not likely, she thought, Lady Ledsham shopping for apples.

'Sophie,' she said, her colour coming back. 'How are you?'

'I'm fine,' Sophie said. 'And you?'

'Fine,' Mandy answered, glad she had got her dark suit on and had had her hair cut and restyled. These days you might not have known her, so different was her lifestyle – her thinking.

Sophie approved of what she saw. This was a different Mandy, quite unlike the image of the cleaning lady she carried in her mind. A swift observation at the cut of Mandy's suit, the make-up and the hairdo, the expensive handbag. A little bitterly, she recalled the generous settlement but she was by nature a kind young woman, and although twenty years Mandy's junior, still had a healthy respect for her.

'Look,' she said. 'Fancy a coffee?'

Mandy took the bull by the horns.

'Yes, that would be nice. Where shall we go?'

'Pity they don't have one in here. What about the corner coffee shop – the Green Door? Half an hour? Fifteen minutes?'

Mandy was anxious to get the meeting over with. 'Say twenty minutes – see you there, then.'

She did no more shopping, but joined the queue to pay her bill, seeing Sophie at the other checkout, and decided that the sooner she got this over, the better. It was bound to happen sometime.

She ordered coffee and sat waiting and soon Sophie appeared. She had put her shopping in the car while Mandy, who had not much shopping, put the plastic bag on a chair together with her handbag.

They both sat with coffee in front of them, then smiled across at each other – a weak smile, but nevertheless one that denoted if not friendship, then understanding.

Sophie took a deep breath. 'Well, I suppose this was bound to happen sooner or later,' she said. 'I wonder we haven't bumped into each other before.'

'I don't come to Oxford very often,' Mandy said, Even her voice was slightly different, more ladylike, Sophie thought, or was that imagination?

'Well, tell me how you are,' she said.

Still, Mandy thought, in charge of the situation.

'I am very well,' Mandy said, 'and how are you?'

The conversation was stilted, as Sophie knew it would be, and she decided to break the ice. It was ridiculous, skating around the edge of things. She always believed in coming to the point.

'How is Tom getting on?' Her eyes were wide and friendly.

'Oh, he is fine. He was twelve last month.'

'Goodness,' Sophie murmured.

Mandy clicked open her handbag, and brought out a small envelope.

Yes, there he was – his features indelibly printed on Sophie's mind.

'He's a handsome lad,' she said. 'A credit to you, Mandy.'

Mandy's face flamed. 'Thank you. He's like his father, isn't he?'

'Yes, he is – like he was at that age.'

Mandy began to relax, deciding that there was nothing anyone could to about it now. She had always liked Sophie – no reason not to be friendly.

'Are you staying with your mother?' she asked. 'At Ledsham House?'

What memories she's got of that, Sophie thought bitterly.

'Yes, I'm staying there – have been for some time.'

'How is your little boy? Andrew, isn't it?'

'He's well. I've left him with his nanny.'

Mandy for the life of her couldn't ask about Lady Ledsham, so instead she asked about Julia.

'Oh, she's fine – pregnant. They've moved up to Shropshire.'

'That's nice,' Mandy said. Although she didn't know it at all.

'So – what are you doing now, Mandy?' Sophie asked at length. She began to wish she hadn't suggested this but it had to be done sometime or other.

'Well, firstly, I've moved house.'

This did surprise Sophie.

'Oh, really – where?'

'To a place called Dudley Court – it's just outside Cedar Green on the road to—'

'I know it,' Sophie said. 'Goodness – that's rather nice, isn't it?'

'It has been turned into apartments,' Mandy said, 'and I bought one of them – a downstairs apartment, the grounds are lovely, and it's quite near the river. It will be nice for Tom to go outside in the grounds and I don't have the worry of a garden to see to.'

That must have cost an arm and a leg, thought Sophie, but then what the hell, this woman was comparatively rich.

'I had to think of Tom,' Mandy said seriously. 'We've been living with Mum all this time, but I had to get out sooner or later for his sake.'

The tension between them suddenly evaporated.

'Oh, I'm so glad, Mandy. You know you look wonderful,' and you could see she meant it.

She thought how pretty Mandy was, at fifty-ish – no wonder her father had found her attractive – but, she thought, a little vindictively, she suspected he had thought that about a great many women. She had had no suspicions before, except those one would normally have about a very good-looking man with plenty of charm, but after the funeral, and all those women there, you couldn't tell her they were all past members of staff. Still, it was water under the bridge now – they all had to face facts.

'I loved your father,' Mandy said suddenly, and for a usually tough girl, Sophie felt like weeping.

'I am sure you did,' she said.

'I suppose I thought he was the greatest thing since sliced bread,' Mandy said, and smiled ruefully. 'When my husband died, I was still quite young, somehow couldn't imagine getting married again – and your father was very kind.'

I bet, thought Sophie.

'I – we – I never thought it would all come out. We kept it a secret for so long . . .'

'You certainly did,' Sophie agreed. 'So Tom has been living with your mother and you all this time?'

'Yes – I moved last week, and it really is lovely. Of course, Tom is at school at Stansford Gate, but next autumn he will be going to Eton. He has passed his entrance exam,' she added proudly. 'I took him – oh, it is such a wonderful school – of course that was your father's idea – he put him down when he was born.'

He would, Sophie thought, a chip off the old block.

'So, life has changed for you, Mandy.'

'Very much so,' Mandy said.

'Have you told him anything about – er—'

'On his birthday, I explained to him – as best as I could. After all, his name is not the same as mine, so I had some explaining to do.'

'What did he say?'

'Nothing – at that age, I don't think it means that much. Or if it does, he keeps it to himself. I told him what a great man his father was.'

'Did he ask about the Ledsham family, I mean, if there were any others?'

'No, nothing. I'll always answer questions truthfully when he does, but I think it should come from him first.'

'Very sensible,' Sophie said.

Mandy was dying to know what Sophie was doing here and how Lady Ledsham was, but couldn't bring herself to ask.

'I'd love to see him,' Sophie said swiftly. 'After all, he is my half brother . . .'

'Yes, I realize that,' Mandy said. 'Well, I don't see why not,' and she saw her opening. 'Would your mother mind that?'

'She's not around,' Sophie said shortly.

Mandy frowned. 'Not around – what do you mean?'

Sophie took a deep breath. 'After the funeral she announced her intention of going away – abroad. She hardly talked to us – you must imagine what it has been like for her.'

'I do,' Mandy said. 'I never thought it would ever come out.'

'You couldn't keep a thing like that secret for ever,' Sophie said reprovingly. 'It was bound to come out sooner or later. It was such a shock to my mother – such a disaster in more ways than one – that she almost went into a decline. We saw little of her, she shut herself away, and then told us she had no interest in Ledsham House – that it would be going to Tom at some point, but that we could live in it if we wanted to – but she had no interest in it. A week later, she had packed and gone.'

Mandy was horrified. 'Sophie! Where is she?'

'We had a card from Paris – then nothing. It's as if she has cut herself off from everyone in England.'

Mandy saw that her eyes had filled with tears. So unlike Sophie, who was the tough one.

She put a hand on her arm. 'Oh, Sophie, I'm sorry. I had no idea.'

'Of course you hadn't,' Sophie said, blowing her nose and pulling herself together. 'How could you? But when things – like this – are done, many people get hurt.'

'In other words, you open a can of worms.'

'Well, I wouldn't put it as harshly as that – still.'

Well, Mandy thought, defending herself, it takes two – and Lady Ledsham— but she wouldn't think about that now. It was all in the past.

'I suppose everyone reacts in the way that is natural to them. Julia is on my mother's side. She always was. I keep most things to myself, but I can understand Mummy's point of view. She was just unable to take it, and dealt with it in her own way.'

They sat for a moment.

Then Mandy got to her feet and picked up her handbag and carrier bag.

'I think I'd better go,' she said. 'It really was nice seeing you. I live at number two Dudley Court – anytime you feel like getting in touch . . .'

'Thank you,' she said.

Mandy could not bring herself to say regards to your mother – how could she?

Head high, she walked towards the cash desk and paid for the coffee, then turned, and with a little wave, left the shop.

Mandy sat on a seat by the river, watching the swans and the eider ducks, the Mandarins with their wonderful colours looking for all the world as though they came straight out of a Chinese opera. This was such a peaceful spot and she was so pleased she had decided to move here.

The apartment was spacious and roomy after her parents' house, and although she hadn't finished furnishing it yet, she knew it would be even better when she had.

Strange how she had ended up here – somewhere she couldn't have envisaged in her wildest dreams. And all because of Tom – the light of her life. She would go through it all over again if it meant that she could give birth to Tom. Not, she thought, that it hadn't been fraught with worry at the time. She hadn't given a damn about Lady Ledsham's feelings – and neither apparently had Robert – the worst thing had been having to tell Edie she was pregnant.

Their rendezvous had been in a little hotel farther up river, a pretty place, hidden, or so they hoped, away from the madding crowds, whenever Robert could manage it. He always had the excuse of being away overnight on business, and she was only too pleased to meet him.

What a lover! Nothing in her married life had given her so much pleasure – although she had loved her husband and was sad when he died so young. But Robert was something else. He knew how to pleasure a woman – she had found that phrase somewhere in a book, and thought that described it perfectly.

When Tom was born Robert was over the moon. 'A son!' he had said over and over again. 'Mandy,' he said, 'I'll give you the moon!'

She smiled now. Well, he had, in a way. Paid for everything, she had the baby in an exclusive nursing home in London, he had paid her a good allowance – there was nothing Tom wanted for, private schools all paid for. Oh, Robert was so proud of him.

Even now, she could feel no pity for her Ladyship. She disliked her intensely – she only kept on working at Ledsham

House because she liked the girls and the house and of course, Robert.

On reflection, she tried to feel what it must be like to learn, as Lady Ledsham had, the details of her husband's private life, but she couldn't raise any sympathy for her. She was a spoiled woman, who exploited Robert, and Mandy was glad that she had been able to provide a little light relief, as it were.

A man passed by on the towpath with a small dog on a lead, and nodded to her. This was private – the grounds of Dudley Court – he must be a resident. She might get a dog, Tom would like that, and it would be company for her. A boat came by, idling, two women lying in bikinis on deck, the man at the wheel. She could have mooring here, but had no interest in boats. Tom may have, later. It was pleasant, sitting here daydreaming, she had never been nor felt so idle in her life. It didn't suit her, because she was by nature an active woman. But she had made up her mind to do things, learn things, if only for Tom.

She had joined the Cedar Green Country Club, very exclusive, fees costing an arm and a leg, but she would be able to take Tom there to lunch on a Sunday. They also had a keep fit class which she had joined, although she hadn't been yet. She was taking elocution lessons – and she might, just might, take French lessons – after all, when Tom was at Eton she would have plenty of time to herself and who knows they might take a trip to France in the holidays. Robert would be pleased if she did that

'Excuse me – may I?' She turned to find a man smiling down at her.

Shaken out of her reverie, she smiled back at him. 'Of course.'

'Thank you,' and he sat down. He was nice looking, around sixty, and she recognized him as the man who had pipped her to the post at number one.

'Edwin Carpenter,' he said, holding out his hand. 'It is time we met, isn't it?'

She took his hand, it was a firm handshake, she liked that.

'Amanda Davis,' she said, 'although most people call me Mandy.'

'I like Amanda,' he said. 'It's an unusual name. 'You live in number two, don't you?'

He had rather nice hazel eyes, behind tortoiseshell glasses, regular features, and a friendly smile. All this she took in, in the space of a second or two, before looking back to the river.

'Yes, I was lucky to get it – I would have liked the one you have, but you pipped me to the post,' and she smiled to show no ill feeling.

They stopped talking to watch an eight going past, the rowers in unison, such beauty of movement as the oars skimmed the water, every man giving every ounce of his strength.

Edwin sighed. 'Wonderful,' he said, then turned to her again. 'You live alone?' he asked.

'I have a son – he is going on thirteen – he is at day school at the moment – next year, of course, he will board.'

'Wonderful time,' he said, and looked back at the river.

'My wife died two years ago – and I have a family, two girls and a boy. They are all married, but come to stay with me occasionally.'

Which is why he wanted the larger flat, Mandy decided.

'That's nice for you,' Mandy said.

'Yes, I love their visits – don't see much of them. One is in Africa, one in Scotland and the other lives in London. I have five grandchildren – so far,' and he smiled.

The man walking the dog returned from his walk and nodded over to them.

Quite a friendly place, Mandy decided.

'You are a widow?' Edwin asked.

'Yes,' Mandy said. 'I have been a widow for many years.'

'It's hard living alone, isn't it?'

'I lived with my mother for quite some time – but now Tom is older I need somewhere of my own.'

'I think we made a good choice – coming here,' Edwin said. 'It's a beautiful spot – and they converted the house very well. It used to belong to a shipping magnate who built it in the late Eighties.'

'I love it,' Mandy said, 'I always wanted to live by the river.'

'I – we – lived in Stowe,' Edwin said.

'Oh, that's a lovely spot.'

'Yes, we bought it when we first married. But it was too big with the children gone and my wife.'

'You were there a long time, then,' Mandy said. 'It must have been a wrench to leave it.'

'Yes, it was. But you have to move on. Life changes. Then you adapt.'

That's true, Mandy thought. That's what life is about. Accepting and adapting.

'You must come in and see my flat – although, of course, you have already seen it . . .'

'Not furnished,' Mandy said. 'And it makes such a difference, doesn't it? I haven't finished mine yet – but there is no hurry. I'm taking my time.'

'Good for you,' he said. 'Er – how about Friday evening? Is that an inconvenient time? Say six thirty – and we'll have a little something to eat afterwards.'

Graziella had been living at The White House for just over two weeks.

Two rooms were put at her disposal, a large bedroom and bathroom, and the room next door – it was like a small suite. She spent most of the time with her grandmother, but was free to use her own rooms as she saw fit.

It was a perfect arrangement, for she spent most of the time with Lady Somerville, but when her grandmother rested in the afternoon had the time to herself. She took to walking into the village, or even going into Oxford sometimes with the car. It was as unlike the life she had lived in Rome as anything could be – but she found a strange pleasure in being with the old lady, perhaps because it brought her own father nearer to her. She had been so fond of him, and the fact that this was his background was fascinating to her.

She had received no welcome from Mrs Baker, but then she had not expected it.

She explored the house from top to bottom, curious as to its design.

'Did my father ever live here?' she asked her grandmother.

'Yes, briefly – when he was at Oxford – we moved soon after he left Eton from Worcestershire, since this house belonged to my husband's family. We moved here, and he came too, of course, but he was soon off on his travels. He was a great traveller, you know.'

Graziella wondered what he had done for an actual living,

for she never remembered him working. Her mother, as an actress, yes – but her father?

It took time to settle in, for life was very different here – but there was a certain fascination about it. For one thing she had no money worries – the money from the sale of the apartment in Italy was ample for her to live on. It was as if she was part of the family now – not a visitor or paying guest.

She got on well with Edie, liking her, but Mrs Baker was something else. She disliked her, sensing that Mrs Baker objected to her being there.

She was always on hand and helped her grandmother with certain things, things that Mrs Baker had used to do. Took her nightcap up to her, sometimes read to her, like a child, slowly but surely becoming one of the family.

As time went by she suggested tidying the cupboards and wardrobe in Lady Somerville's room. Books, books, masses of them, sometimes she read bits out of them, dusting them, putting them away. Tidying shelves, she was indeed a companion.

One afternoon, while Lady Somerville slept, she walked through the village from end to end. Saw all the shops – remembered some of the people she had met at that fabulous garden party, introduced herself to Greta Nelson in the dress shop – they had a long chat, talking of Italian fashions. It quite made Greta's day.

Another time she went out for coffee and walked along to Laura's shop, where she went in, reintroduced herself, and they had quite a talk, Laura being impressed with this beautiful woman who had come to live in Cedar Green.

Now that she had got used to the idea of being Lady Somerville's companion – as indeed had Lady Somerville – Graziella thought more and more of how she could get rid of Mrs Baker. With Edie doing an extra half-day, she was sure they could manage. But would her grandmother be agreeable?

One afternoon, on Mrs Baker's half-day off, they sat beneath the chestnut tree, drinking tea, and eating cakes which Graziella had made.

'These are delicious,' Celia said. 'Did you bake them?'

'Yes – I am quite a good cook.' She had cooked for her mother but she didn't tell the old lady that.

'Excellent,' her grandmother said.

'I must get some more water for the teapot,' Graziella said, getting up. 'I had forgotten it was Mrs Baker's half-day.'

There, she had spoken her name – now it would be easier to bring her into the conversation.

When she returned, having dealt with the pot, she poured more tea, and helped herself to another small cake.

'How old is Mrs Baker?' she asked.

'How old?' Celia repeated. 'I have no idea – she must be sixty . . .'

'Yes, I imagine,' Graziella agreed. 'She has not been looking at all well lately.'

'Really? I had not noticed,' Lady Somerville said.

Well, she wouldn't, Graziella thought, with her eyesight, and she probably hasn't really looked at Mrs Baker for years . . .

'Sometimes, I wonder if—'

'What?' the old lady said sharply.

'Well, it would be nice if we were – I mean, now that I am here to take care of you . . .'

'You are not here to take care of me,' her Ladyship said sharply. 'You are my guest, my personal companion.'

'That's what I mean.' Graziella said easily, 'if Edie could do another half-day, I know I could manage. I would love to run this beautiful house – and I love being with you.' She reached over and took the old lady's hand.

Lady Somerville's eyes filled with tears.

'Oh, you are such a nice girl, Graziella,' she said. 'I wish we had met years ago – but still, better late than never.'

She had sown the seed, Graziella thought happily. A few more reminders at the right time . . .

Nineteen

When Janet and Pat Mackay turned up together on Tuesday morning, Laura was somewhat surprised.

'Hallo, great to see you – everything all right?'

They sat down looking as if they meant business.

'I sold two more watercolours,' Laura said. 'He must be good, Derek—'

'Oh – Derek is it now?' Pat laughed. 'That's the stuff – the more friends you have the better.'

'Shall I make us come coffee?' Janet asked.

'Please, Jan,' and she disappeared into the kitchen.

A customer came in, interested in the old desk, while Pat joined Janet in the kitchen.

'I don't know if this is such a good idea – to tackle her now,' Janet whispered.

'Either you like the idea, or you don't, and if you do then there's no time like the present,' Pat said.

The woman having gone, with a promise to come back with her husband, the two women rejoined Laura.

'Well?' Pat asked.

'She is interested in the desk,' Laura said. 'Going to come back with her husband.'

'Good,' but Pat was never one for beating around the bush, and she waded in. 'Janet has a proposition for you.'

'What?'

'And if you don't like it just say so,' and she sat back with her coffee.

Janet chose her words carefully. 'Laura, I'll come straight to the point. I would like to come into the business with you.'

Laura was flabbergasted. 'What?' she almost shouted.

'Well, I have to have something to do before I sell up, and it seemed to me that you can't really cope on your own in this business, no one could, what with—'

'I know all that,' Laura said impatiently. 'I need help – and I am grateful to you both.'

'No, it's more than that – I wondered what you would think of the idea if we shared the business as partners. I'll put my share in and we will share the profits, the work, the hours.'

Laura's thoughts were whirling, and she was tempted, nevertheless – without thinking it through.

'Just a minute, Jan – this is a complete set-up. I mean, living accommodation, business—'

'Well, I don't want the living bit – although when I sell up and you could have lots of my furniture – I mean, *we* could have . . .'

Laura could not deny that she needed help, for she couldn't be in two places at once – and a permanent partner sounded a good idea.

'And you go along with it?' she said to Pat.

'Yes, don't look at me to make a threesome – I am happy doing what I am doing. Besides, I couldn't afford it.'

'No one asked you to,' Laura said sharply, hoping she wasn't being manoeuvred.

'Jan, dear, I know you've been through a bad time, but have you really through this through? Think what it entails . . .'

'What am I to do with my life? I might just as well go into partnership with you.'

'You make it sound like desperation point,' Laura said.

Pat intervened. 'Look you two need to calm down. Jan has made a perfectly harmless suggestion, that the two of you go into partnership – why not?'

'Because the living accommodation and the garden is all part of it.'

'I don't want the garden.'

'No, but I do – and that's all part of it.' Hmm, Laura thought irritably. Why had they come along now just as she was getting settled? But she wanted to help Jan out of a tough spot – was this the way? Could not Janet help her out as she had been doing?

She suggested this.

'Dear Laura, I want to get involved with something – anything to take my mind off the situation I am in.'

'When it's resolved you may change your mind?' Laura said.

'I might buy you out,' Janet said with a false laugh.

'Well, let's say you're doing well,' Pat conceded. 'I can't see anything wrong with the idea, sounds perfect to me.'

'Oh, it would to you,' Laura said, as a customer came in and the women made themselves scarce in the kitchen, washing up the coffee cups, muttering under their breath.

They reappeared when she had gone, and got down to business again.

'Look, think it over again, the two of you – and when you come to a decision that you really want it, I'll have a word with John – John Paynter – my solicitor.'

The other two exchanged glances.

'Fair enough,' Janet said. 'You're not annoyed, are you?' she asked Laura.

'Course I'm not – it was just such a surprise.'

Graziella was having her early afternoon walk while her grandmother had a rest. She intended to go to the bank, and there was a small branch at the end of the High Street.

She had just closed the gate behind her, when a man stopped, almost bumping into her.

'Oh, I am sorry.'

She had seen him before – wasn't he the man with that awful woman from Heron Court?

'No damage,' she said, smiling what she knew was a rather special smile.

'I know you, don't I?' the man said. 'We met at the garden party in July,' and he held out his hand. 'Benjamin Green.'

'Graziella Massini. I am Lady Somerville's granddaughter,' and she made up her mind at that moment that she would change her name by deed poll to Somerville.

'How nice to see you – are you going my way?'

'I am going to the bank,' Graziella said.

'I am going that way, may I accompany you?'

'Of course,' Graziella said, while he couldn't believe his luck. He had thought never to see her again – such a beauty.

'You are staying with your grandmother?'

'Yes.'

'I am just going to drop these letters off at the Post Office – so seldom these days with e-mail and all.'

'Yes,' Graziella said, not sure if she was pleased or not at meeting him. Still, a tall, handsome man, middle-aged – and, so she believed, one of the developers at that large house – well.

'How is the work going?' she asked, trying to keep in step, and he slowed down, aware of the slim high heels tripping by his side, and those legs.

'Slowly at the moment – excuse me,' and he posted the letters in the box, coming back to her. 'May I come with you? I will wait outside, then perhaps we could have a cup of tea at the Cedar Tea Rooms?'

That would be nice, Graziella thought. She was hungry for a man's company.

'I won't be long,' she said, as the small bank appeared and he waited whilst she went in.

Her business was soon accomplished, and she met him again outside.

'Have you ever been here?' he asked, as they approached the small café.

'No, but I expect it is typical of a village tea rooms,' she said.

It was pleasant inside, one or two people, and a woman came forward to present the bill of fare.

'Tea?' he asked.

'Please,' Graziella said. 'Earl Grey – I have got used to it in the past weeks, and I must say I quite like it.'

'Anything to eat?' the woman asked.

'Well, do you know, I am going to have a scone with jam and cream – my grandmother tells me that is the best thing about English tea.'

'Then twice,' Benjamin said.

The woman disappeared. How out of place they looked, she thought, although they had so many tourists, she was used to unusual people.

'Earl Grey for two – and two scones, butter and jam,' she called over the serving counter.

Graziella and Benjamin smiled at each other.

'So tell me,' Graziella said, 'what do you do?'

'I am a developer – of building sites.'

'Oh, are you one of the people who are going to build at Heron Court?'

'The same,' he said smugly. 'That is my firm, I am a director, although my nephew owns it – Greensward is the name.'

'How interesting,' Graziella murmured. 'May I ask what will happen to it? Lady Somerville and I drove along to see it quite recently – it is a beautiful house.'

Ever keen to talk about his business, Benjamin waded in. Explaining the pros and cons of English development and the difficulties.

'But I think it is the same everywhere. Heron Court lends itself to such a development – we have already done three retirement homes, most successful.'

'I think I met the owner – is it Mrs Hastings?' she asked. 'At the garden party,' she added, by way of explanation.

'Yes, we were there,' he said. 'Great, wasn't it? A lot more goes on in these villages than you might imagine.'

Graziella smiled.

'So you haven't started yet. What will Mrs Hastings do? Will she stay on in one of your fabulous apartments – they do sound interesting,' she said, to soften her question.

'Oh, no, I don't think so. Soon she will have to move when the building work gets too much for her – it is quite a big development.'

'I imagine,' Graziella said softly.

'And how about yourself?' he asked. 'Are you just on holiday?'

'Oh, no, indeed,' Graziella sounded shocked. 'I live with my grandmother, Lady Somerville.'

'Ah, yes,' he said softly. 'Another scone?'

She smiled. 'No, thank you, one is quite enough, but I will have another cup of tea.'

Thus ended their brief sojourn, and he walked back with her to The White House, where he leaned over and opened the gate.

'This, of course, is the most beautiful house in the village,' he said. 'In fact for a long way around. Georgian, of course, probably one of the first houses here.'

He leaned forward. 'Can you imagine what it is worth now?'

She had often wondered, but looked shocked. 'No, indeed I can't.'

'Well, I cannot tell you what it would fetch on the open market – make a beautiful hotel, too. Well, signora . . .'

Graziella smiled.

'Graziella,' she said, and looked up at him with those eyes. How had he ever thought Vanessa was a beauty?

'I hope we meet again,' he said, and left Graziella standing at the gate.

Lady Somerville was sitting in the front window, awaiting Graziella's return. She was furious when she saw who she was with, and when she entered the room, turned swiftly.

'Who was that you were with?' she asked in a fearsome voice.

'Benjamin Green, the developer,' Graziella said coolly. 'I met him – bumped into him just outside the gate.'

'I should give him a good miss,' her grandmother said. 'Such people—'

'I'll just pop upstairs and take off my jacket,' Graziella said, going over the last piece of their conversation in her mind.

Worth a lot, eh, a hotel – well, the chances were there. She was pleased she had decided to come and make her home in England. The possibilities were there – she had known that. And it all came from having a grandmother like Lady Somerville. Her own family, she thought, her own kith and kin.

'I've got masses of homework tonight, Daddy,' Janie said, making for the door, .

'Well, get going,' John said.

'And by the way—'

And then the phone rang.

'Yes, hallo, Laura.' Janie hovered by the door.

'Yes, by all means . . . tell you what, call round this evening – can you do that? Around eight, we'll have a chat about it . . . see you then . . . bye now.'

When he looked over at the door his eyes were warm and smiling.

'Now off you go,' he said. 'No reading until late.'

'No, Daddy,' she said, and once outside the door, punched the air.

'Yes!' she said, and ran up the stairs.

Twenty

Fifteen minutes later, Laura had arrived at Churchgate House. John answered the door to her, and held out his hand, leading her in to the hall and thence to the sitting room.

'Sit down, my dear – is something troubling you? That's what I am here for.'

He sat down opposite her.

'Well, not exactly troubling me . . .' He saw her smiling now, but there was a frown between her eyes, and he felt he wanted to comfort her.

'Well, I'll begin straight away. Janet Weatherall and Pat Mackay came to see me this morning, and Janet, who has been through a hard time lately—'

He nodded. He had an idea what was coming.

'Well, to cut a long story short, Janet said she would like to come in with me – in the business, on a fifty–fifty basis.'

He was surprised. He knew how desperate Janet felt about her future, but had not expected this.

'A drink?' he said, feeling the need for one himself.

'Well, a little sherry or wine – I don't mind either.'

He took his time, allowing her to relax, then took the glasses back with him from the sideboard.

This was a sticky problem, but he had many worse than this in his life.

'Presumably she means the business side of it – not the house nor garden – the lease and what it entails, I imagine – a share in the actual business, then?'

Laura looked relieved. 'Yes, that's it – she is not interested in the whole lease; as you say, a share of the business.'

'Well, this could be a bit complicated, but it could be worked out. Floating it as a company with so many shares each is a bit large for such a small concern, but you could do it simply. Come to some arrangement, but it would have to be legal – that she takes a share of the losses as well as the profits.'

'Oh, yes,' Laura said.

He secretly thought that Janet was probably a better businesswoman than Laura – Laura belonged in her garden.

'By the way, are you enjoying it so far?' he asked.

'Yes, I love it – it's the rushing about though, as soon as one thing gets sold I have to replace it, and that means getting out and buying.'

She sipped her drink. 'That's where Pat Mackay comes in handy, she is such a help – brings things in. And Janet will have lot of stuff when she sells up.'

He made no reply. Janet Weatherall was a client and it was not for him to tell another client of her plans.

'Well, Laura, let's deal with the share of the business. If you would like me to, I will draw up some ideas for you to look at, and you will see what it entails for you both. How would that be?'

'Oh, how kind of you, John!' She looked relieved. Poor little thing, she appealed to him, sometimes he felt he wanted to take her in his arms and comfort her, but reminded himself that she was a businesswoman – a client.

'I will pay you for this visit, John,' she said.

'Oh, good Lord! If I can't do something for a friend . . . Besides, you are busy most of the day, so an evening visit works very well. How is it coming along?'

'Quite well,' she said. 'A few customers – sold a few things. Sold a super picture the other day for quite a big sum.'

'Good,' he said. 'And how is the garden coming along?'

And now her eyes did light up.

'Oh, John! It is wonderful – with these light nights it means I can get out there, it is such a bonus.'

'And how is Jamie?'

'Coming home next weekend,' she said. 'I shall be so pleased to see him. He has been travelling around Europe with his friends.' She put down her glass. 'Thank you so much for seeing me, John. It's wonderful to have a friend when in need.'

'Do you want a lift back?' he asked.

'Heavens, no!' she said. 'It is a lovely evening.'

And when she had gone, he missed her.

* * *

Not having seen much of Benjamin Green in the last week, Vanessa decided to go up to town to visit the studio room she had taken in Bayswater to store her bits and bobs. Looking around, she wondered whether, after all, she might be better up here in London. It was more her style – not here, of course, but somewhere more exclusive, an apartment in Holland Park, for instance, Chelsea might be too expensive, the magic triangle of Belgravia far beyond her purse. Today she would stay in the studio, as it was called. There was a single bed which might be useful. Go to the agent's and have a look round.

She quite enjoyed her day and saw several flats which might be suitable, took the agents' particulars home with her to read and study. Getting out of the station car park, she drove back to Cedar Green and Heron Court.

She almost wept when she saw it – this is where she belonged. Here was her home, but it wasn't any more. Still, if Benjamin Green came up to scratch, and they lived in one of the better apartments, she would be part owner of the development – but somehow she couldn't see it coming off. And to live in part of Heron Court was not the same thing as owning it as a residence.

She could do better than that.

Resting from her day out in town, she made plans.

The upshot was that she invited John Paynter out to lunch. To thank him, she said, for all the work he had done on her behalf when poor Stuart died. After all, she owed him that. He had been a good friend – and a good solicitor. Smoothing her path through the sale, the Greens' lawyers – yes.

John Paynter was not that surprised to receive an invitation from her – and judged that it might be somewhat difficult to refuse. She was the widow of his best friend, so it was logical to accept – but he was not looking forward to it.

'That's very kind of you, Vanessa. I should like to . . . er, which day do you have in mind?'

'Friday – or any day to suit you.'

'Then Friday it is. I will pick you up, Vanessa,' he said. 'Twelve thirty? Where did you have in mind?'

'Well, since it is a special occasion – La Grande, at—'

'Vanessa! There is no need for that, surely?'

'If I am asking, then that's where I mean,' she said. 'We have never done this before, John, and we have something to celebrate getting out of a difficult period in my life, so we are celebrating.'

There was no answer to that and he felt a little like the lamb being led to the slaughter.

When the telephone rang in Lady Somerville's house, she answered it. The call was for Graziella – Signora Massini – a personal call from a man called Benjamin Green.

Celia had half a mind to put the phone down, but realized she was being childish, and went on to say she was not sure her granddaughter was in.

But there was no help for it; Graziella passing through with the tea things quickly grasped the situation.

Her grandmother handed her the receiver, and wheeled her way out of the drawing room.

Graziella was not best pleased to receive the call – she liked to keep her affairs private – but now the ice was broken, she decided to go along with it.

'Is it possible you could meet me in Oxford one day next week? I have some business to attend to in Oxford and would like you to join me for lunch, if that is possible?'

'Which day is that?'

'Wednesday next.'

'I think that might be arranged,' she said. 'I will telephone you on my mobile phone.'

'I didn't know you had one,' he said, pleased as punch. That would ease things more than somewhat.

'Shall I pick you up?' he asked.

'Yes, please – leave it to me, just tell me the time.'

'Twelve,' he said.

Celia met her in the doorway a frown on her face.

'Benjamin Green?' she said. 'Isn't he the developer at Heron Court?'

'Yes, darling, he is, but he is going to help me with the papers – you know, naturalization and changing my name, all that – I haven't a clue.'

'My solicitor would have done that – John Paynter. He is a very good man.'

'I never thought of that,' and Graziella's pretty face looked so abject, that Lady Somerville wheeled herself over to her.

'My dear, it doesn't matter – I only wish I could go with

you to help things along. I was forgetting how much is involved
– after all, you are an Italian citizen.'
  'But not for long!' Graziella cried, and she looked so pleased
that Celia soon forgave her. All the same – that man – she
had not liked the look of him at all.

Graziella looked wonderful when she was ready to go to lunch,
but Celia was getting used to that. She never, ever looked
anything but beautifully turned out, or had a hair out of place,
yet it was natural to her – a born beauty, her grandmother
decided, born with a flair for fashion.
  Benjamin Green thought so too, as he held the door open
for her to get into the car, and soon they were on their way
to Oxford.
  They sat in the bar of the hotel drinking, totally at ease
with each other, although they had nothing in common.
  'So you grew up in Rome?' he said. 'Wonderful – I envy
you.'
  'My mother was an actress – and my father, well, as you
know, was Lady Somerville's son.'
  She was quite reserved in her conversation, and he guessed
that there was a lot behind it.
  They were called to the dining room, elegant and welcoming.
  'So,' he said, after they had ordered. 'You are no longer
married?'
  'Unfortunately, no,' Graziella admitted. 'I say that because
I thought it was for life – such is a young girl's dream, living
happily ever after – but it was not to be.'
  Her lovely eyes looked into his. 'And you?'
  'I have been married twice,' he said. 'The first when I was
too young, we both were, straight out of college, wanting to
live our own lives. It only lasted eighteen months, and then I
met Sue – we lived together for a time, then married, and
after that – well, it fell to pieces. She was ambitious, a lawyer,
and she worked all the hours God sent, and loved her work,
I thought I was better out of it. So . . .
  'Sad in a way – one hopes for so much, when you embark
on a marriage – then . . . Still, I don't intend to remain a bach-
elor for ever.' He smiled, and took her hand across the table,
and she didn't take it away until the waiter arrived with the
desert.

Looking at this young woman over the table, her beauty, her charisma, he wondered how he had ever, ever, considered Vanessa Hastings attractive. He hoped with all his heart that she would soon settle somewhere. It embarrassed him to think he had led her up the garden path. But he had meant well, and knew in his heart that he was a fool where women were concerned. But he couldn't go wrong with this one – no man could.

By the end of the week, Graziella had persuaded both Mrs Baker and her grandmother that Mrs Baker needed a rest – a break, from what seemed to Graziella a hard-working existence.

Well, Mrs Baker had to admit, she had not been feeling all that well lately, and perhaps a week or so with her sister in Bournemouth might be a good idea. As long as her Ladyship could do without her . . .

'Of course,' Lady Somerville said. She had thought two weeks earlier in the year was sufficient for what she called a housekeeper, even with all the things Mrs Baker did for her, but now that she had her adored granddaughter, things would be different.

Once she had gone – at least temporarily – Graziella relaxed again. Free at last, with Edie doing an extra half-day she knew she could manage. Had she not taken care of her mother all these years? She felt she could breathe again.

Vanessa settled on a flat in Holland Park. It was expensive, but then she had money – and given time, she knew she would find a man, certainly in this part of London, which she remembered from her youth, and the man was more likely to be suitable than someone from the countryside. After all, who would she meet there?

Benjamin Green sprang to mind – but she discounted him. She had had hopes at first, but on reflection decided that he was too much involved with her past life at Heron Court. She must not hold on to her past, but find a future. She was still young – well, young enough to be presentable – and she knew how to play the field.

She would return to Heron Court, and tell him that at some point soon, she would be moving out, back to London – he was not to know she had not lived there since she was a girl. And what business was it of his, anyway?

Cut your losses, everyone advised. Was that not the expression? Well, that was what she was going to do.

'Auntie Barbara,' Janie said, stopping at May Tree Cottage on her way home from school. 'I would like to talk to you for a moment – are you busy?'

She was at the sink, her back to Janie.

'Darling, I am always busy, but I always have time to talk to you. Is something worrying you?'

'No, not worrying me – but I wanted to tell you, Laura, Mrs Grey, came round to see Daddy last night.'

Barbara was all ears, although she didn't turn round.

When Janie didn't go on she turned to face her.

'Well?' she said. 'So?'

'Do you think – I mean—?'

'It was a business thing, I expect,' Barbara said, although she was interested. 'You must remember Laura doesn't have much time to herself during the day.'

'She didn't stay long.'

Barbara dried her hands.

'Now, Miss, what are you getting at?'

'Nothing. Nothing – I just wondered . . .'

'What?'

'Auntie Barbara, do you think it possible that Daddy and, well, you know, Laura, could . . .?'

The thought had crossed Barbara's mind several times, but then it had with several different women but nothing had come of any of them – it had all been her imagination. John had shown no inclination for any of them.

Poor little soul, she thought. How she misses her mother – and come to think of it, was Laura a possible stepmother?

She grew quite warm at the thought of it. But with that blessed shop – that was the only thing she was interested in. More's the pity.

John Paynter stopped outside Heron Court, waiting for Vanessa to join him. The times he had done this, waiting to drive Stuart to a game of golf – but all that was past history. Now he could scarcely believe that less than a year since Stuart had died,

Heron Court had been sold, and he was about to take Stuart's wife out to an expensive restaurant – except, of course, that she was taking him.

She was on time, dressed exquisitely and had an expression in her eyes he had not seen there for a long time.

He started up the car.

'Vanessa, nice to see you – you are looking very well.'

'Thank you, John. I am feeling well – and looking forward to our lunch.'

'What have you been doing with yourself?'

'Ah, something very interesting. I will tell you over lunch,' and his heart sank. He always dreaded those heart to heart talks with Vanessa.

But at least she looked bright – and chirpy was the only word.

She said little on the journey, as though savouring what she had to tell him till they were seated in the bar of the hotel.

It was a wonderful day, the gardens all around filled with flower beds, a fountain – and well-dressed visitors taking aperitifs in the sunshine. For some unaccountable reason he thought of Laura Grey – and wished that she was there with him. How different it could have been.

'Well, John,' she said, sipping her dry Martini, her eyes wide and friendly.

'It sounds as if you have something to tell me,' he said.

'I have, John, I was going to save it for lunch – but you might as well know now. I have given a lot of thought to my future – bleak though it is – and I have decided to go to London to live.'

He was shocked but pleased. Best thing she could do – and had a great sense of relief.

'Really? You surprise me. When did you decide this?'

'I have had quite a lot of time since the sale of Heron Court went ahead – and I must do something with my life. It is no good trying to emulate what it was, that's over and finished – you know how I felt about Stuart.'

I do indeed, he thought grimly.

'And I must make a fresh start – cast adrift, away from all this.'

'And where will that be?' he asked.

'Holland Park, in town. I lived there once before, as a single woman, and I know the area – although it has changed more than somewhat. I have bought – or I am buying – a flat.'

He felt his heart burst with relief.

Thank God – as long as she was around he would think of his dear friend Stuart Hastings. Now, he would not have to worry about the tragedy of it all.

'Will you need help from me, as your solicitor?'

'That's sweet of you, John, but I shall change my solicitor to town – no point in having one out in the sticks. Well, I don't mean that, but—'

'I understand,' he said. 'I imagine you have enough money to see you through?'

'Money – oh, yes, John, I have now,' she said, 'enough to buy the apartment – it is a long lease.'

'Oh, well done, Vanessa,' he said. He couldn't be more pleased and knew he was going to enjoy his lunch.

Twenty-One

S adie knocked on the door of the little cottage, and it was quickly opened by Edie.

'May I come in for a minute, or are you just going out?'

'No, come in – I'm not due at Churchgate House for another quarter of an hour. Like something, Sadie – tea or coffee?'

'No, thank you, Edie. I thought I would call in and give you some news – unless, of course you've heard it?'

'Depends what it is,' Edie said, and grinned.

Sadie sat herself down.

'Well, it seems that Vanessa – your Mrs Hastings – is moving to London . . .'

'No!' Now Edie was surprised. 'Really? Who told you?'

'My brother, Benjamin.'

'Well, I would be the last to know,' Edie said. 'Still, I'm glad. I always thought it best that she moved away.'

'So did I!' Sadie said fervently, and Edie laughed.

'Yes, I know you would be pleased, but it's best all round – too many memories round here for her, too many changes.'

'Oh, I am not thinking of her,' Sadie said.

'No, I didn't think you were,' said Edie, and she laughed. 'Anyway – everything all right?'

'Fine – now,' Sadie said.

Edie stowed something in the fridge, and turned to Sadie.

'I thought of something when I was slicing beetroots – do you remember borsch, the beetroot soup your mother gave me?'

Sadie looked puzzled. 'Beetroot soup? No, I don't remember . . .'

'She said I looked thin, wanted feeding up.'

'That sounds like Mum,' Sadie said. 'What a hoot!'

'I remembered it this morning – where are you going this afternoon then?'

'Moreton-in-the-Marsh,' Sadie said, 'to speak on the values of vitamins in your diet.'

'Well, you are doing a great job – and keeping yourself occupied.'

She put on a cardigan and picked up her handbag.

'Well, let's go,' she said.

On Tuesday Laura came downstairs and unlocked the door to the shop. It was a warm morning, and she left the door open to attract customers.

She flicked a feather duster around and had not been there more than half an hour before Pat Mackay, staggering under the weight of a large cardboard box, came in, looking pleased with herself.

'You've been busy,' Laura said.

'Yes, I went to an antiques fair on Saturday and picked up quite a few things. Well, I'll show you, and you can see if you are interested.'

'While you unpack, I'll put the kettle on,' Laura said, then closed the outer door.

On her return, Pat was half unpacked.

'I don't do books,' Laura said, eyeing a rather splendid blue leather-bound book of J.M. Barrie's plays.

'Yes, you do. The odd book placed carefully on a table – very tempting. This is a first edition – 1928.'

'See what you mean.'

'And this is a rather nice Sèvres plate – and here we have a Noritake teapot and hot water jug on a dear little tray. Very pretty and very much collected now.'

Well, she would know, thought Laura.

'And here is a black Cartier evening bag – see, here is the label inside – and you know what handbags are fetching now.'

Slowly she unearthed the contents of the box – including a large Coalport meat dish.

'I also found, which pleased me more than somewhat, a dear little Victorian chair – a child's chair but I am afraid I am keeping that. I have a weakness for tiny chairs, children's that is, don't ask me why . . .'

She was an unusual person, thought Laura, but very useful.

'Oh, and five little Delft dishes – not a crack anywhere – what about those?'

Each was wrapped separately in tissue.

'Oh, you are good,' Laura said.

'Now, what I will do, what I have done,' Pat said, 'is to write a list of the things, and what I paid. You can ask what you like, but that's my price guide. And that is what I want, my money back.'

'But where's your profit?'

'Oh well, I just hope you sell them at a good price. If you do, you may give me a tip.'

Laura sat long after she had gone, and had coffee, until she took the things into the kitchen. Pat had already washed them all, and referring to the list, she sat down and priced them.

It was quiet this morning, and towards midday Laura began to accept that this was going to be one of the quietest days she had had, when the door opened, and a tall man entered the shop and came across to where she was sitting at the desk.

'Good morning,' he said. 'Mrs Grey?'

'Yes?' she said. Somehow he had an air about him.

He held out his card.

Reading it, she saw 'Graham Swann Private Investigator' with an address in London, and for some reason she thought of the actor with the silver.

She handed it back. 'How can I help you?' she asked, but her heart missed a beat. It looked so ominous.

'I understand that you sold a painting recently – a portrait of an unknown woman, an Edwardian Lady, by the artist Edward Boone?'

'I don't know who the artist was,' Laura said.

'It was signed – but perhaps not somewhere you would look for it. Did you ever have it out of its frame?'

'Not to my knowledge,' Laura said.

'Ah, well, it is by Edward Boone.' She waited. 'And the sitter's name is Angelina.'

'Is there a problem?'

'I am afraid so,' he said. 'It happens to be stolen property.'

Laura was stunned.

'But it can't be – it has been in my family for about twenty-five years to my certain knowledge. I inherited it when my father died.'

'But it is still stolen property,' he said. 'It was stolen from a house in the early Sixties – from a house in Marlborough, where my client's parents lived.'

'Your client – and who is that, may I ask?'

'A Mr Robert Smith,' he said.

Laura tried to pull her thoughts together. Oh yes, she remembered him. Funny how she had thought there was something odd about all that.

'The sitter was Mr Smith's great-grandmother. It was signed – 1910 – by Edward Boone.'

She could almost feel her hands beginning to shake.

'Do you know where your father purchased it?'

'From an art gallery in Cheltenham I should imagine – I really don't know much about it, it was left to me by my parents when they died and it has hung in my house ever since. I lived in Belford before I came here,' she said, hoping to establish her innocence, and as if it mattered.

'Nevertheless,' he said, 'it is part of the proceeds of a robbery in the early Sixties,' and he glanced around as if to find further evidence of stolen property.

'Do you know its provenance?'

'I am afraid not – as I've said, it came down to me when my father died, together with other things.'

'Your father was a collector?'

'Yes, mainly of antiques but the odd picture.'

'Have you among his papers, perhaps, details of where he bought that particular painting?'

'No, nothing like that, all his private papers – I have all his family documents . . .'

'Do you suppose the receipt for purchase could be among those?'

Laura thought not – she had got rid of most of the stuff she had thought unimportant at the final move she had made from Belford. There had not been room for anything more than her personal important documents.

'No – I kept nothing. Birth and death registrations, all that sort of thing, family achievements and photographs – but I don't recall seeing any receipts for purchases of antiques. It was a long time ago . . .'

What right did this man have to question her on her family? Oh, John, she thought, John Paynter – help me! And she recalled he had thought it was an Edward Boone – was he into fine art? How did he know what it was?

'Still, the provenance is important in a work by an artist like Edward Boone.'

'I told you, I had no idea it was by Edward Boone – and if I had it wouldn't have meant anything to me. I'm sorry to say, I was just selling on something that I owned that I no longer wanted.'

'But you put quite a high price on it – three hundred and seventy five pounds.'

'That's not a lot today in the art world,' she said quietly. 'And I am not exactly a moron – I could see it was a good painting, otherwise my father would not have bought it.'

He studied her for a few moments, then laid down his card.

'I will leave this with you,' he said, 'and you will be hearing from me again.'

Her heart was thumping oddly when he left, and she could not be more grateful to see anyone when Janet Weatherall opened the door, the little bell rang, and a call – 'Coo-ee!' – brought her out of the kitchen.

'Oh, Janet!'

'What's up?' Janet said. 'Whatever's the matter? Calm down,' and she put an arm around her shoulder.

Calmer now, Laura told her story, and the more she told Janet, the more furious Janet became.

'Bloody cheek!' she said. 'I hope you told him where to get off!'

'Janet!' Laura cried. 'He was a private investigator – hired by these people who bought the picture!'

'Rubbish!' Janet said. 'The Smith man is trying it on.'

Laura opened her eyes wide.

'Trying it on? In what way?'

'He wants you to give him his money back – it's a scam. He probably does it all the time.'

'Janet, but this man – Swann—'

'They're in it together – and all I can say is they would have a fight on if they were dealing with me.' And she sat back, arms folded, determination in every part of her body.

While I, thought Laura miserably, am scared to death of anything like this – my darling father, a thief! She felt like weeping, but in front of Janet? Never!

'What now?' she asked.

'Phone John,' Janet said. 'You need a solicitor.'

Oh, I do, thought Laura, I do.

'What do you mean – scam?' she said presently.

'Oh, I don't know – a try-on. That man, the purchaser, knew that you were new to the business, if he scared you enough, you might give him his money back and let him keep the picture.'

'No way!' Laura cried.

'I am very glad to hear it,' Janet said, in her practical way. 'You should hear what Pat Mackay would have to say about it!'

'What?'

'Well, she would be sceptical, like me.'

'I am going to give John a ring,' Laura said.

'Yes, you do that – I'll tidy up a bit.'

After the telephone call, John asked her to be at his house by eight o'clock – he and Janie would have finished a meal by then, and he and Laura could relax.

When he opened the door to her, he could see she was so het up, she could hardly speak. She had been worrying about it all day.

He held out his arms, and she went into them. 'Oh, John!'

'Laura, my dear!' He held her close, feeling the warmth of her, and the slight trembling of her body – something indeed had upset her.

Still with his arm around her, he led her into the drawing room, and seeing she was comfortable, went off to fetch them a drink.

'Drink this,' he said, 'and tell me all about it.'

She didn't need the drink to spill out what had happened, and his eyes grew stern.

'The suggestion that my father stole it – was a thief – I can't bear it!'

'My dear, no one is suggesting that.' He waited for her to calm down.

'Are you sure you haven't anything of the history of the stuff you were left?'

'No, there might have been bills and receipts, but I suppose when I moved from Belford I got rid of everything – couldn't see how I needed any of his personal papers.'

He sat thinking. 'I thought it was an Edward Boone,' he said slowly.

'Yes, you said – but I'd never heard of him, I am afraid I am not into art – in that sense.'

'But you knew it was a good picture.'

'Oh, yes, I knew that much.'

'And of course, a genuine Boone would fetch much more than that.'

'Really?'

'Yes, even though this man wanted it for personal reasons – at least if we are to believe his story – he's on to a good thing. Anyway . . .'

'Then why rake this up?' She raised anguished eyes to his.

'The first thing we must do is to contact the local art shops and galleries in Cheltenham – that's if any of them are still there. It is a long time ago – would you like me to take this on?'

'Oh, please, John.'

'Very well, I will do all the searching I can and let you know how I get on – I have a good man in mind.'

He sat thinking.

'Did you bring this man's card with you?'

She delved into her handbag.

'Hmm,' he said, reading it.

'I can't bear that anyone would think my father stole the picture,' she said. 'He was quite a well-to-do man, and collecting was his hobby.'

'I am sure,' he said.

This had really stunned her, he thought, as nothing else had.

'I'll run you home,' he said.

'Thank you, John.'

He had never seen her like this – and through his mind ran the thought that really those other two women were more suitable to run a shop like that. She had not been open long, and already there was a problem – and you had to have a business head to deal with that, whatever there was behind it.

Outside her house, he went towards the front door and she handed him her key.

Opening it, he allowed her in, then put his arms around her.

'Will you be all right?' he asked.

Oh, John, she thought, if I could stay like this for ever, I would be.

'Yes, thank you, John,' and he kissed her lightly, before closing the door behind him.

He was amazed at the depth of his feelings – he hadn't felt like this for, well – since Lyn was alive.

At the end of three weeks he had to report that nothing was known of a painting by Edward Boone in any Cheltenham gallery.

'What now, John?'

He took a deep breath.

'Have you heard from the private investigator chap again?'

'No,' she said. 'Not a word.'

'Well, perhaps you won't,' he said. 'But I don't think that's the end of it. The man I hired is good – he has enquired not only in Cheltenham but all over the place.'

'Oh, you are so kind – but it hangs over me like a threat,' she said. 'I can't concentrate.'

'Of course it does,' he soothed. 'Look, why don't I come round and see you tomorrow evening – does that suit you?'

'Oh, yes, John – thank you.'

But she couldn't sleep that night. Tossing and turning, as the hours went by. Not so much about the picture, but John – John Paynter.

Was that what she wanted? A man to comfort her, put his arms around her – soothe her – was that it? A father figure?

But she was reminded of emotions and feelings she had felt, oh so long ago, when she had met her husband. They had been young, headstrong, both of them – beautiful people – he was so good-looking, and out of all the girls who admired him, she was delighted that he chose her.

They met at university – stubborn young people, both sets of parents against an early marriage, but they wouldn't listen. And then what?

It hadn't taken long, even before Jamie was born, for her to find out that he had other women, other girls. Just couldn't keep away from them. Was born to it – and she, young fool, had not seen through it.

Well, that was what she was, wasn't it? Headstrong,

thoughtless, never thinking things through, like the shop –
thank goodness there had been someone like John Paynter to
comfort her. Was that all it was? But deep down she knew
she felt more than that. Not just the comfort of a big man to
hold her, but desire, too, and strong affection. Was that love?

She plumped the pillows angrily and turned over again.
Switched on the light – to find it was three thirty.

She must be mad. And what about John? He might have a
lady friend – lots of lady friends, a mistress even. Of course
he consoled her – that was what a kind man did. She wished
he had kissed her properly, and imagined it – she hadn't had
such thoughts since her husband left . . . over and over again
. . . and then Janet, with her strength, her fury, at the picture
business – wanting to share the shop – oh!

But Jamie would be home this weekend – how glad she
would be to see him! She had only stayed married for Jamie's
sake, deeming it necessary for a boy to have a father – but
what a father. Her own father had been like a father to the
boy. Jamie adored his grandfather, he had taken him everywhere, on boats, visits to museums, on holiday – he had adored
him – when he died it broke Jamie's heart.

And suddenly she sat up in bed, her heart pounding as she
remembered her father's briefcase. Jamie had asked for it
when he died. 'May I have it, Mum? It's special to me.' That
lovely leather briefcase with her father's initials in silver on
the front, and she leapt out of bed and into Jamie's room,
banging her knee on the door in her haste, reaching up to the
top shelf in the cupboard where Jamie kept all his books and
papers and private things – and there was the briefcase.

She lifted it down, it was heavy, and throwing it on the
bed, unlocked it, emptied it out on the bed and out spilled
masses of papers, photographs, permits, licences, certificates
for this and that and a large roll of papers in a rubber band.

Her heart was pounding with excitement, her hands
everywhere.

She went through the papers like someone demented, and
then the roll – she slipped off the rubber band, and flicked
through the papers like a roll of banknotes and there – she
could hardly believe it – were receipts.

A receipt dated May 1976, for forty pounds, for a painting
by Edward Boone. ANGELICA – and from an art gallery in

Edinburgh, Scotland. She read it twice, before clutching it to her, leaving all the contents on the bed to clear in the morning. The bedside clock said four thirty, as she slid beneath the bedclothes, still holding the receipt.

Then she slept.

Twenty-Two

A year after the death of her husband, Diana Ledsham was packing her bags once again to fly out of Italy and back to Paris, where doubtless her travels would begin all over again. It had been the most boring year of her life, one hotel being much like another, and the men, once you got to know them, equally boring. After a few days in Paris, she thought she might try Chamonix – or Sicily.

This time was a little different. She no longer had Nicole Deschamps with her, the maid she had hired. She had put up with enough of her stupid chatter about the women she had previously worked for and now was on her own.

It was late afternoon as she came through the swing doors of the Hotel Crillon, and she struck, as she always did, an arresting figure. A porter followed carrying her furs, another her Vuitton luggage, and the man sitting idly in the reception area reading his newspaper glanced up, down, then looked again. If he wasn't very much mistaken it was Diana Ledsham.

Not much interested him these days, but the sight of Diana Ledsham did. No sight nor sound of her for over a year, and here she was in Paris. His large, square face flushed slightly as he wondered how best to approach her. Not now, but later, since she was obviously staying here – but for how long?

His heart quickened with interest, and he felt hot under the collar. He watched as having booked in she would obviously be staying here. But for how long? After she had gone to the lift, he made his way to the reception desk, and on the pretence of collecting his keys and his mail, idly read the register upside down. The last entry was sure enough, Lady Diana Ledsham, with an address in Italy. That, he knew, was their small private villa. Had she been there all this time?

He went straight to the bar and ordered his drink, taking it to a table where he could see straight through the great doors to the reception area. Later he would have dinner but he wanted to be sure that he did not miss her. She was unlikely to go out, having just arrived, but he wasn't going to miss this opportunity.

Just before eight o'clock, he saw her emerge from the lift looking ravishing. Exquisitely dressed, her head held high, she looked neither to the right nor to the left, but went straight to the dining room where a waiter led her to a discreet corner, and she would have her back to him, he realized when he took his seat.

No matter – he would know when she left, and it was at that point that he determined to speak to her.

Her back straight, hair perfectly coiffed, her slim arms and beautiful hands with their dark painted nails, the rings flashing – oh, yes, it was Diana all right. Where had she been all this time? He had caught a glimpse of that expressionless face but strangely enough the cold expression did nothing to spoil her beauty, rather enhanced it. Her face might have been carved out of marble.

He ate his meal, his mind on other things, and when he had finished took his coffee in the coffee lounge, which he knew she would have to pass through. If she didn't stop, he would accost her. Yes, quite openly. If she sat for coffee, so much the better.

He was playing a waiting game, but speak to her he would.

She came through from the dining room and took her seat on one of the soft single armchairs with a table before it. Only when the waiter arrived with the coffee did she move to pick up the cup. The coffee black and strong, she was looking straight in front of her.

She was still beautiful, he thought, but then women don't lose that kind of classical beauty, and those wonderful eyes, she could be blind for all it mattered, so dead was the expression in them.

He got up at once, and made his way across to her.

She was forced to look up at the dark shadow in front of her, and he saw a flicker in those eyes.

'Jack Leadbetter,' he said softly. 'Diana?'

He saw that he had startled her, but her composure was excellent.

'Jack,' she said. 'Jack Leadbetter!'

'May I?' he asked, and brought a chair alongside hers before she had time to object.

Well, he decided, she's not the woman she was, but then I'm not the Jack Leadbetter I was. We are two different people.

She said nothing until the waiter brought more coffee, then she asked him, 'Susan not with you?'

'Susan? Oh, well, of course – you've been away. Susan and I are divorced.'

This did register and her eyes widened.

'I'm sorry – I didn't know.'

'Why be sorry?' he asked. 'It was inevitable,' and I'll tell her, he thought, if it's the last thing I do. She's so bloody placid, looks as if nothing could touch her – leaving those girls, clearing off like that. Susan may have had the morals of an alley cat but she was warm – this woman is like ice. She cares only for herself. Jack was a simple man – there was nothing devious about him.

They drank their coffee, saying nothing, then he turned to her.

'I always like a little stroll after a meal.' He saw her frown. 'It's a lovely evening, Diana – want to come?'

He saw she was about to say no, then she took a deep breath.

'Well, a little way – a breath of fresh air . . .'

'That's it,' he agreed. 'Shall I get you a wrap?'

'No, I'll be fine,' and she drew the soft silken scarf around her shoulders which matched her dress.

They walked out of the swing doors and into the streets of Paris, the soft night air about them. Presently he took her arm and she made no demur, seemed rather grateful.

She was only a little thing, he thought, feeling a momentary outrage against Robert and what he had got up to. It couldn't have been easy – still . . .

They walked silently until they reached the Seine, and stood looking down into the dark waters, with brilliant lights everywhere and riverboats and lovers, Notre Dame standing high and proud. I came here with Susan, he thought, but it was difficult to know what Diana was thinking. It always had been.

She shivered slightly.

'Shall we go back?' he asked.

She nodded.

They walked back slowly, he having said none of the things he had meant to say.

Once inside the hotel, it was warm, and he made straight for the sumptuously furnished lounge.

She sat on one of the soft sofas.

'I think we need something cheering,' he said. 'A brandy?'

'Please.'

After the waiter brought the brandies and she had taken a sip, he decided the time had come.

'Well, what have you been doing with yourself?' He wouldn't chide her, wouldn't criticize her actions; only she knew why she had done what she had.

'Travel, mostly,' she said, as if she was unused to speaking.

'And where have you been – anywhere interesting?' He tried to sound light, mildly curious.

'All over, Italy, Switzerland, Venice.'

'Is Venice still as beautiful?'

'I suppose,' she said languidly. 'I didn't care for it as much as I used to.'

And he took the plunge.

'Well – you and I are not the same people, Diana.'

She turned to look at him.

'What are you doing here?'

'I had a spot of business to do, then thought I'd stay on for a couple of days. And you?'

She took a deep breath. 'A stopping-off ground – before I—'

'Whiz off again?' he asked.

'Yes – I expect so.'

No good asking after the girls – they hadn't heard from her. She was always a selfish bitch, he thought, but looking at her saw that she was also vulnerable, and what she had learned that day at the funeral would have given some women a nervous breakdown. But then it had, in a way.

'Diana,' he said, 'isn't it time you faced up to a few facts?' After all, he had nothing to lose.

She looked coldly at him.

'I'm better not knowing,' she said. 'I already learned enough to last me a lifetime.'

'Yes,' he said, 'but life goes on,' and he took the plunge. 'Did you know that Susan was or had been Robert's mistress?'

'I suspected,' she said calmly.

'You mean—?'

'Jack, you can't be married to someone like Robert and not know.' And she knew it was the first time she had said Robert's name out loud since he had died.

'Susan adored him.' She looked at him. 'All women did. Poor Jack.'

'I had no idea – until it all came out – over this other chap.'

'People like Susan, and Robert, should never marry. They can't stay faithful . . .'

'But if you knew, why did you—?'

'I never realized how many – there were so many – and then of course . . .'

'The boy.'

'Please don't talk about it, Jack. I can't bear it.'

Now the violet eyes were full of tears, and he welcomed them. No one could see them, and he wouldn't have cared if they had. This was Paris, where emotions were not something to be ashamed of.

'But I held on to him – all those years.' It was proudly said.

She stared ahead. Yes, he thought, with all your little illnesses – your little dramas. Robert always thought you were so frail, like a broken flower – had to be taken care of, while he lusted after other women. Sick kind of life, Jack thought.

And now, her face seemed to crumple, and she reached for her handbag and her hankie.

'I'm sorry, Jack. Forgive me.'

'Look,' he said. 'Let's take you to your room.'

She made no demur when he took her arm, and they went over to the lift. Once inside the room, he poured her a cool drink of ice water. 'Drink this,' he said.

Now, the violet eyes had a trace of warmth in them as she looked at him.

'Oh, Jack you don't know—'

'I can imagine,' he said. 'Don't talk anymore.'

She sat on the chaise longue.

'I think I am going to faint.'

'No, you're not,' Jack said, causing her to open her eyes wide. 'You're strong, Diana, and don't you forget it. You may not look it, but you're tough – and you know, that's something to be proud of, isn't it?'

She got up and went over to the window, where she stared out into the lovely courtyard, where a fountain played and tubs of flowers shone their colours in the gleaming night lights.

'I'm going home at the weekend, Diana,' he said. 'Will you come with me?'

She turned, startled, then her shoulders sagged, it was as if she suddenly collapsed inwardly.

She smiled at him. A lovely smile. 'Yes, Jack, I will.'

Twenty-Three

B ack in Cedar Green over the little antiques shop, Laura awoke and looked at the bedside clock, and was shocked to find it was five fifteen, and thought for a moment it must be afternoon. She felt surprisingly clear headed, and remembered in a moment flooded with relief that she had found the missing receipt – she was still holding it in her hand.

Oh, and she felt like crying and laughing at the same time with relief. She hadn't the slightest desire to sleep anymore and lay quietly contemplating the past few days' events.

She would telephone John first thing – he would be relieved, she knew he would, and fell to thinking about her life as it had been up to now in Cedar Green.

She had a strong desire to examine very closely her decision to open the little antiques shop. She had wanted to so desperately, she accepted that – but was it really for her? When she thought of how well Janet and Pat Mackay dealt with things – had she really the temperament for running a business? Trading? Bargaining? Selling? Janet and Pat seemed to take it in their stride, and things like the stolen painting were a challenge to them. She had felt simply awful, and not fit to deal with such problems. Was she doubting her ability because Janet was keen to buy into the business?

She thought not. If she were honest with herself she would admit she was not cut out for it. The wonderful furniture her parents had left her she could imagine in an antiques shop. She had been desperate to find a new life for herself after Jamie had started university, had done courses in fine arts and attended lectures – yes, she had been interested, still was. But was she really cut out for the retail side of it? The part she liked best in her new life was the gardening at weekends. That part came naturally to her – but was running a retail business for her?

She had to do something with her life – but was it this?

She liked Janet – she was a true friend, and she certainly would not give in to both her and Pat Mackay taking over the shop – being in a partnership was not her sort of thing. It was all or nothing for her.

She had thought all along that John Paynter did not approve of her doing such a thing – but what had it been to do with him? It was her wish, and she had had no second thoughts about it – until now. Now if it had been a little house with a garden – she would have loved it. Anything to get away from that house in Belford where she had first lived with her husband. Too many memories.

But she had thought that was right too. Made a decision to marry, had not seen through the deceptions – the other side of him that was drawn to women and always would be. She respected him as a man and father to her beloved son – but nothing more. They had been drawn together, so young, and marriage was inevitable. These days you would live together – which might have been better for them. Then the agonies of divorce wouldn't arise. How did you know if you would make the same mistake a second time? First her marriage and now the shop – was she incapable of making the right decision?

And now what was she thinking? Her face flushed as she thought of John Paynter. Yes, there was no doubt she had fallen for him. He was so comforting, such a man, straight – you would never connect him with secret liaisons, other women. But what was she doing thinking of John as a second husband?

But how could she trust herself? She'd made a mistake in her marriage, then she had wanted an antiques shop and now she was fed up with that. What would have happened if Janet had not been interested? She would have been forced to carry on. But for how long? Already she had doubts that she had made a mistake while her two friends seemed admirably suited.

The business had worried her more than somewhat – and if she were honest, having to go out to the auction sales and the deliveries and so on – was it really her thing? Whereas Janet and Pat Mackay took it in their stride.

But she wasn't lazy, she knew that. Could pull her weight with anyone. But business, trade – that was something else.

You had to have a head for it, she remembered her father saying.

But how to solve it. Even if Janet took the shop over, it was her home. She loved her new kitchen, the whole area – where would she go if she didn't have the shop?

No – she must be strong, and carry on. John would work something out.

The next morning Laura telephoned John before he left for the office.

'John, I've found it – the receipt!'

'Good God! Are you sure?'

'No doubt about it – you are coming round this evening, aren't you?'

'Yes, I am looking forward to it – Laura, that's wonderful!' He could imagine how her eyes were shining.

He'd had a long day at the office, one of the difficult days, but he showered and chatted to Janie, asking about her day.

'I am off to see Laura,' he said casually after they had eaten. and saw the gleam of satisfaction in her blue eyes.

'Oh, give her my love,' she said.

'I will,' he said – and thought, I would like to give her mine. But we will see.

Janie watched him drive away, and waved. Were they an item? she wondered. Not yet, perhaps, but they could be, and she hugged herself. Oh, if only.

Laura appeared at the side door where he parked his car, and he knew everything was all right by the expression of relief on her face. Once inside, the gate closed, he hugged her, then quite deliberately, kissed her, and she felt she never wanted it to stop.

'Oh, John,' she said at length.

He was much taller than she was, and stood looking down at her, at her flushed face, the shining eyes, the smile – of relief? Partly, he thought, but hoped because they had found each other.

She took his arm. 'Come in,' she said.

Once inside the house, he kissed her again and held her tightly. Yes, she was the one. He had met many women since his dear Lyn died, but this one – she was the only woman who had moved his heart. Was he mad? He had thought her slightly batty when they first met – now he didn't care if she was. He wanted to look after her.

She took his hand. 'Come in – I have something to show you,' and she brought out the precious bit of paper, the receipt that meant so much.

He read it – and hugged her again.

'Where did you find it?'

'You will never guess. In the middle of the night, I couldn't sleep, and I remembered that Jamie had asked if he could keep my father's old briefcase when he died. He was so fond of him – and I flew into his room hauled it down, and there it was, in a roll of receipts, bills, purchases and so on.'

He looked down at her. She wasn't as tough as Janet Weatherall, but she would be strong when she had to be – and she was not in the least like Lyn, his dear departed wife, but he was excited at the thought of marrying her, and knew Janie would be too. He had no doubts that she would accept him. He could read genuine feeling when he had to – they would be good together. Besides, she loved gardens didn't she?

They were married in October on a lovely day, a gift of a day, in St Martin's Church, in Cedar Green. Practically the whole village was there, it was a very happy occasion, and no one more pleased than Janie. Barbara too – she was delighted to see her beloved brother married again, and dabbed her eyes over and over again at the ceremony, and she wasn't given to tears. Janet Weatherall was part owner of the shop now, and Pat Mackay helped out. John was happy – *She'll give it up altogether soon*, he thought – *just let her free in the garden, and she will find no time for the shop*.

The bells rang out in Cedar Green – it was a very happy occasion.

In November Lady Somerville was taken ill. The doctor thought she'd had a mild stroke, and from then on they watched her carefully. Graziella was a devoted nurse, looked after her every minute, read to her, told her stories about her father – even mentioned her mother, but that brought no response.

Graziella sat by her bedside, read to her, held her hand. She had grown so fond of the old lady – more than she had thought possible.

But the end was near, and one morning in December, going to her room, Graziella found that she had just passed away.

She wept, knowing she was going to miss this wonderful grandmother she had found so late in life. Almost everyone came to the funeral, she had been quite a character in Cedar Green.

After the funeral, when John Paynter read the will, Graziella discovered that apart from bequests to charities, Edie and Mrs Baker, Lady Somerville had left everything to her beloved granddaughter, The White House – and a great deal of money.

Before her grandmother became ill, Graziella had been seeing quite a lot of Benjamin Green. After all, she liked a man's company, had even thought of marrying him – she knew he wanted that. But now it was different.

Marry Benjamin Green?

She would be mad to do so.

Now she was somebody, not Lady Somerville – but Graziella Somerville, the owner of The White House, and you couldn't say fairer than that.

Surely, nothing less than a title would suffice?